The Matchmaker's Report

RUBY D. FLOWERS

Copyright

Chapter One

The door slammed shut, bumping Rachael's back heavily. The bags she carried threatened to spill all over the worn, floral carpet of her Mimi's living room.

"Careful baby," MiMi Palmer called from the kitchen. "You know we're on a fixed income. You best not have broken my good olive oil."

Grappling with the plethora of plastic, paper, and reusable bags that she had so painstakingly strategically placed on her limbs, Rachael managed to get all the way inside the house without spilling.

"Your olive oil is fine, Mimi," Rachael said with a weary sigh. "Don't worry, I'll bring them in one bag at a time. I know it's precious cargo. If I break it, I won't be able to get any of your famous broccoli and garlic pasta or that good olive oil cake."

"You know that's right! Now come over here and give me some sugar," MiMi said.

Rachael wrapped her grandmother in a hug, careful not to squeeze too hard or bump the walker that MiMi used to keep her upright at the stove. Every Wednesday, without fail, Rachael went from her job at WCP Industries to the grocery store to do the weekly shopping for her grandparents. Two things she could always count on- MiMi , cooking a delicious dinner, and Pops Palmer devouring it before jokingly asking when the real dinner would be served. The other guarantee was that her grandparents would be able to distract her from whatever fresh hell her boss, Mr. Hendrick Pfeiffer, had come up with over the course of the week. For the last few months, Rachael had persevered through a series of teambuilding challenges that were extremely inappropriate, all orchestrated by her boss, who also happened to be the CEO of WCP. In his all-knowing brilliance, Mr. Pfeiffer had partnered her with one of the worst men in the company- Peter Kane. He was a sleaze. Her skin crawled just thinking of how much time she had to spend with the handsome jerk.

"Now let me take a look at you." MiMi adjusted her glasses and pulled back so she could get a better look at her grandbaby. She brushed her dainty fingers over the shaved side of Rachael's scalp. "When are you going to grow this hair back? How are you going to get a man with a half-shaved head and the other side-dyed... what is this color? Electric blue and purple?"

"I'm not looking for a man, Mimi. I only have room for one man in my life right now, the only deserving one anyway," an image of Peter at the last team event, grinning at her rakishly, briefly flashed in Rachael's mind. "And that man is sitting in the den watching reruns of *What's Happening* and *In the Heat of the Night*."

Mimi chuckled. "Your Pops is a handful, but you know we won't be around forever, and I want to see some great grandbabies before we pass on to the great beyond."

"You two aren't going anywhere. I don't even like to think like that," Rachael said. "Now, what did you get up to today?"

"Don't change the subject. Now, when was the last time you went out on a date and spent some time with a man?"

Once again, unbidden, Peter's unwanted face popped into her mind. Rachael shook her head and shrugged. "We're in the 21st century. I don't need a man. I'm thinking of going full 4B anyway. You want me to get that pot for you?" Rachael asked, getting up to bend down and get some cooking utensils from a lower cabinet.

"Ummhmmm. I saw that look. Changing the subject won't save you. You have someone on your mind. Now, I'm not going to push you now, but I want you to tell me about him if things get interesting."

"There's nothing interesting to tell, and there's not going to be. He's an asshole. Honestly, men like him are why women-"

"Language!"

"Sorry, Mimi."

"Thank you, baby. Now stop telling me about women and tell me about this, asshole. He sounds interesting! You know, some ladies just love an asshole. It's all they want, an asshole-ish man."

" MiMi Palmer! You kiss your grandbabies with that mouth? I couldn't say it, but you've said it like three times in one sentence," Rachael teased.

"I can say it. I'm Mimi. That comes with privileges. You get to be my age, and you can say a whole lot of things. Asshole, being the least of them. Now tell me why this man is such an asshole, or is he the whole ass?"

"He's really not important. Just this guy that I've been partnered with for leadership and team building for the entire year. He just thinks he's the hottest thing walking. Stole the fiancé from a friend of mine and flaunted it all over the office. He didn't even want the girl. Then he has the nerve to taunt my friend, Casey, with it at one of our events." Rachael moved around the kitchen, taking the knife from her grandmom, and began smashing the garlic and tossing some whole cloves in olive oil for roasting. "It ended up in a fistfight. I was so embarrassed and I'm kind of worried that Casey may get disciplined. Seriously though, Peter deserved what he got."

"Sounds hot and fiery. You know, those kinds of men make the best lovers." MiMi said as she sat down, fanning herself and winked at Rachael. "You should go for him."

"Eww, Gross! Nothing about that sounds appealing."

"I'm just saying a bad boy like him could grease your cogs." MiMi grinned at her and took a sip of her tea.

"Mimi... just... no," Rachael groaned.

Slow, labored steps could be heard coming down the hallway.

"Bess! What are you doing to my baby girl?"

Pops Palmer entered the kitchen, his once broad shoulders and straight back now bent forward and supported by a cane. His bushy grey brows were shadowed by thick-rimmed glasses that magnified his mirth-filled, sharp, brown eyes. He cut a path to the stove, lifting lids and sniffing the contents of the pots.

"John, don't you come in here looking for food and for trouble. I'm not doing nothing. I'm trying to get us some great-grandbabies!"

"Grandbabies?" His eyebrows rose above his frames. "Not my Rachael. She ain't but a little bit. She's not grown enough for babies."

"She's thirty years old. Plenty old enough. Shoot, we had three kids by the time we were her age. One of them, her mother, mind you, was almost a teenager."

"Yeah," Pops turned to Rachael, giving her an exaggerated wink. "That's only because you were fast. You couldn't resist my charms."

"Man, you better get outta my kitchen, calling me fast. Like you weren't there, too!" MiMi swatted at Pops's backside with a pot holder and giggled.

"Alright now, Bess. I'll go, but not without getting a little taste first." Pops leaned over, wrapping his arms around his wife of fifty-five years, and gave her a long kiss on the lips, leaving her utterly breathless. MiMi slipped back down into her seat, unconsciously fanning herself and watching her man walk out of the kitchen.

Rachael glanced back and forth between her grandparents and smiled.

"Everything good, Mimi?"

"Woo! Too good. See that right there? That's what I want for you. Spicy and feisty even when they are old and grey. You ought to give that boy a chance."

Rachael started to respond, but MiMi cut her off.

"You don't need to say anything, but just think about it. He may be an asshole, but oftentimes, that may be a defense mechanism. There's usually more to the person. And if there isn't, well, no one ever said you can't just have a bit of fun until the real deal comes. Now let's get back to cooking."

With that MiMi ended the discussion, and the two returned to their regularly scheduled evening of cooking, eating, and loving.

Chapter Two

THURSDAY

Thursday morning found Rachael groggily racing through her morning routine. She awoke to the frenetic jazz grooves of Thelonius Monk. She sprang upright in bed, rubbing her eyes, trying to encourage her spirit to move as quickly as her body just had. Once she had convinced herself that this was indeed real life, she was able to get through her ablutions and whip up a batch of her extra special, all-natural organic, super-food adaptogenic green smoothie. She poured the smoothie into a large thermal cup, grabbed her keys, bag, and helmet, and headed to the door. Her cat, Risky Business (Risky for short), meowed loudly as she tried to leave.

"Listen, Risky, I'd love nothing better than to stay home with you, but Momma has to make these dollars if you're going to keep up your catnip habit," Rachael said.

Risky just meowed even louder as he rubbed against her legs and started weaving in and out, preventing her from leaving.

"What is it? You know I have to go." Rachael asked as she continued to the front door. Risky jumped on her side table and used his paws to knit up and down against her arm. Finally, he leaped up onto her shoulder and swiped at her head.

5

"Damn, sometimes I wonder about you, Risky. You give serious dog energy." Rachael reached up to grab her cat, who immediately leaped off her shoulder. Instead of touching his fluffy fur, she came in contact with the cool satin of her bonnet.

"Whew! I can only imagine what folks would have said if I rolled into work with my bonnet still on. Thanks, Risky."

She arrived at the offices of WCP, scooter helmet in hand, just in time to grab the elevator before the doors closed on its trip up to the fifth floor. She took a moment to center herself and do some breathing exercises. Nothing calmed her like her deep, controlled breathing. Except on this particular Thursday morning, she couldn't relax into the exercises because, on her first intake, she caught a whiff of a familiar citrusy, juniper, cinnamon, woodsy scent. Her inner peace was shaken as she realized that she was on the elevator with her partner and team building nemesis- Peter Kane.

"Morning, little bird." Peter's deep voice sent chills through her body. Whether it was from the previous night's conversation with MiMi or simply that she hadn't had time to steal herself for an encounter with Peter, Rachael couldn't decide. His 6'3" muscular frame crowded Rachael in the too-small space of the elevator.

"I've told you already- do not call me that. What is your problem, man? It's not even eight in the morning, and already you're not right."

"Why not? You adorn yourself in the plumage of a strutting peacock, and you make such sweet little chirping sounds when you are trying to be feisty," Peter said and booped Rachael on the nose.

Rachael felt a flush of hormones run through her body. She felt agitated and insulted by his words and condescension of his "boop."

"Oh, you... you're such a jerk!" She turned her whole body toward him, fist balled, and started to rush up to him. "Who do you think you are? You don't get to call me anything other than Rachael or Ms. Palmer."

Peter just chuckled and relaxed his stance even more, leaning against the elevator wall, hands in pockets, one leg casually crossed in front of the other. He looked like a model leaning against a wall in Italy for a GQ spread. His slightly pouty mouth quirked in a pleased smile. The knowing look he gave her as she felt herself becoming unreasonably angry keyed Rachael up even more. She started to move forward, invading his personal space.

"Listen you, you're nothing special. Just because people around here call you handsome and you were able to break up a happy home," Rachael emphasized her words by poking him in the chest. "Doesn't mean you can swan around here and do or say anything you want. I'm not one of those girls who thinks you're just so handsome-"

"So you do think I'm handsome," Peter retorted and placed his hand over hers, holding it close against his chest.

"Ugh! You just don't listen, do you?"

The elevator dinged and came to a stop. The doors opened, and another passenger joined them.

"My, my.. hehehehe."

Rachael's internal voice screamed. Any other morning, she could take the elevator to the fifth floor alone and uninterrupted. Not today though. No, today she had to have Peter join her and the very worst person, her boss, Mr. Hendrick Pfeiffer.

"You two look cozy," Mr. Pfeiffer said. Hendrick Pfeiffer was the founder and CEO of WCP Industries. He was a handsome silver fox of a man with a mischievous nature. He was always up to something it seemed. He had questionable ideas of how to build a team. He had already subjected his chosen leadership team to rounds of middle school-level party games. He was the reason Peter felt so comfortable teasing Rachael.

"It's not what it looks like, Mr. Pfeiffer," Rachael squeaked.

"Oh? It looks like you two are having a very private conversation. I mean, Peter is holding your hand close to his heart, is he not?"

Rachael realized that Peter hadn't let her go yet. In fact, as she tried to pull away, his grip tightened slightly, and his grin turned into a full smile.

"Hendrick," Peter gave the CEO a confident bro smile, "Rachael was just explaining to me my proper position in the company. It was just a mild disagreement."

"Ah, I see. Well, I'm sure you two will figure out a way to make everything work. I don't want two of my rising stars that I hand-picked to be leaders, to be anything but a cohesive front." He looked the two of them over, his piercing eyes making contact with both of them. "Or would you prefer that I get involved? I could mediate. I do love a challenge."

Rachael looked at Peter pleadingly before finally being able to yank her hand away from his chest.

"Uh, no, sir. We have this. It was just a minor misunderstanding. I really appreciate the opportunity you've given me with the Leadership Jams. It's been a wonderful opportunity." Rachael's words scrambled over one another in an attempt to make up for any ground lost by Peter's admission that they were having a disagreement.

"I certainly hope so. This is where I get off. Have a great day, and if it can't be great, make it spicy." Mr. Hendrick Pfeiffer exited the elevator, giggling to himself.

Once the doors closed, Rachael seethed in silence.

"Oh, Mr. Pfeiffer... it's not what you think, sir," Peter imitated in a high-pitched, ingratiating tone. "Are you afraid of Hendrick?"

"I'm not listening to you, so don't waste your time mocking me. I actually want to keep my job. I don't need to have a target on my back. Especially not because of *you!*"

"Me? How am I the problem?"

"How are you not the problem? I'm not the one taunting people and getting into fist-fights. You need to check yourself. Look, I don't have time for this- it's barely 8:00 A.M., and I haven't had time for my smoothie, let alone a cup of coffee. We haven't even gotten off of the freaking elevator yet!"

Rachael reached down and picked up her forgotten helmet and bags from the floor.

"Seriously, just leave me alone until the next team event in a couple of weeks. We don't need to interact with each other for any other reason."

"Rachael, I-" Peter started.

The elevator dinged, and thankfully for Rachael, it was finally on her floor. She couldn't remember the last time a five-flight elevator ride took or felt so long. She backed out of the elevator and waved to Peter with her free hand.

"Bye, Peter. Get your act together."

Chapter Three

Peter sat in his office with the door shut for most of the morning. He needed to quiet his mind. Riding in the elevator alone with Rachael had both been a pleasure and a pain. Any time alone with her tweaked something inside of him that had lay dormant for most of his life. Rachael was the kind of woman that he was drawn to by the tenth degree. She was lean with long, curvy legs that he was certain would look good wrapped around his waist. Her hips were slim but contained the sweetest, roundest bubble of a butt. He wanted to sink his teeth into that bubble. With a trim waist and pert, full breasts, Rachael was physical perfection. Her punky, tough girl aesthetic was merely the icing on the cake. However, even without being perfect to look at, Rachael was brilliant. Peter remembered her resume coming across his desk as part of the interview team when she had been a young applicant five years ago. Even then, she had made quite an impression on him.

It was true that he had spent his time at WCP test-driving many of the women in the company. It was just a bit of fun and never anything serious. They all knew the score- he was never going to be the settling-down type. He was fun and had good looks. He knew he was arm candy, and he liked it that way. He learned early in life that women were nothing but trouble and that he had to control the situation at all costs. Keep it flirty, fun, and sexy. Get your kicks and keep it moving. He still couldn't understand how he had let things get out of control with the last woman. That's what the fight had all been about. To him, Kerry Dennis was just another trick. Sure, he knew that she had a fiancé at the company, but it shouldn't have been a problem to have a little fun. Keep his pipes clear while she went off and played happy family with that Casey guy. He had no problem with the guy- he was a good co-worker and seemed like he would eventually move along in the ranks. It would have been perfect- Casey would have all of the responsibility, and Peter could be the jump-off for when she wanted a little extracurricular fun, a little bit of strange. It was never meant to get out of hand the way it did. Sure, he had needled Casey a bit at the last team-building event- a game of Twister, of all things, but how was it his fault if Casey took things too seriously? How was he the problem?

Rachael was a problem. He wanted her, sure, he wanted any pretty woman. The thing was that he liked teasing her. He wanted her responses, whether it was laughter or irritation. These days, she was more irritated than anything else, so he did what he could to get a rise out of her. He wanted to hold space in her mind, even if it was only agitation from his juvenile flirty antics.

Peter's musing was interrupted by the buzz of his phone. He picked it up and saw his father's name on the screen. He felt a full-body cringe as he debated answering. Better to deal with his dad now and get it over with while he could use his job as an excuse to end the call early.

"Yeah, Dad," Peter said as his greeting.

"Yeah, Peter," his father, Evan, mocked, leaning heavily on the last syllable of his name. "Is that how I taught you to speak to me? No, hello, how you doing? Just 'yeah,' like I'm you're dog?"

"Sorry. What's up, dad? It's good to hear from you," Peter grumbled as he rolled his eyes and logged on to his computer.

"I can't just call you? Something has to be up?" Evan's voice pitched higher, his tone indicating he was about to ramp up into a rant.

"Dad! I'm working."

"Yeah, yeah. Okay, okay. Your little sister is starting after-school classes at the academy. I promised her she could." He left the statement hanging.

"Which one, dad? You know I have three little sisters. Caroline's daughter? Sadie's daughter? Or my mother's daughter? You have so many I can't keep up."

Peter could hear his father's irritated breathing.

"Emma. Caroline's kid. What does it matter? One of *your* little sisters is taking extra classes. You make the big bucks, Mr. Executive. Help me out here."

Peter frowned and shook his head. This was so typical of his father. Always asking him to pick up the slack for his many dalliances and gambits. He wanted to deny his father for once, but he would be depriving Emma of her chance at one one-on-one ballet training, and it wasn't fair to her. She was really good and had the potential to get accepted into their full-time program. She could become a principal dancer if she had the right training and opportunity. He ran his hand across his face and, against his better judgment, gave in.

"How much?"

"I just need four."

"Four what? Four hundred? No problem."

"No, I need $4000."

"I can't believe you, dad. You promised her something that you *knew* you couldn't afford?"

"I'm on a fixed income. What do I always tell you? Give women what they want. Keeps them quiet and out of your hair. Don't take them too seriously."

"Yeah and you also tell me to get in and get out. Are you going to apply that advice to your own children as well?"

"Don't be disgusting. That's different. Are you going to help me out or not? I'm on a fixed income and a whole lot of child support."

"You could get a job, you know."

"C'mon. Don't break my balls over this. Are you going to let your little sister miss out or what?"

"Fine," Peter said through gritted teeth. "I'll meet you with the money after work."

"Thanks, son. You're a good boy. I'll talk to you later." Evan Kane disconnected before Peter could say another word.

Peter fought to push down the lump that sat in his chest. He absentmindedly rubbed the spot where Rachael's hand had rested earlier that morning as if trying to soothe himself with the ghost of her touch. An email alert popped in the bottom right corner of his monitor.

To: Kane, Peter; Palmer, Rachael
From: Kathy Starnes (on behalf of Hendrick Pfeiffer, CEO)
Subject: Leadership Jam-Side Project

Dear Colleagues,

Thanks to the outstanding progress that you have both exhibited in our team-building exercises, you have been chosen to embark on what I would like to call a "side quest."

Our company is looking to court several new vendors. In order to achieve our goals I would like to have two of my rising stars scout sites and meet with the prospective clients. This will require that you both work intimately together to formulate the correct chemistry to win these clients over. This assignment will last for approximately two months with meetings and scouting happening twice a week.

It is imperative that you demonstrate that you are capable of settling disputes, confusion, and even resolving flaws and misunderstandings that may arise. I understand that this task will include that problem-solving between the two of you as a unit and overcoming any personality conflicts that you may have.

Trust the process. I guarantee that if you two work together, your complementary skillsets will result in a marriage of compatibility and success. Provide a weekly report to me, tracking your wins.

I'm counting on you both. I expect good things.

Sincerely,

Hendrick Pfeiffer, CEO

Peter read the email and smiled.

Chapter Four

CUBICLE LAND

Rachael opened her email and gave a strangled yelp, trying to suppress her reaction unsuccessfully.

"Uh oh. What's going on?" Rachael's work bestie, Chaundra, asked.

"It's nothing. Just a new work assignment," Rachael admitted.

"Must be a real doozy to make you react like that."

"You could say that," Rachael retorted as she backer her chair out of her cubicle so she could speak to Chaundra without shouting over their cubicle wall. "Can I tell you how much I love my job? We have great benefits. I can come in and dress to fit my personality. I get to hang out with you every day. It's great! I know that my skills are appreciated. My brain gets to stretch."

"Okay... I know this is leading up to something," Chaundra prodded, raising her eyebrows.

"It is. Stay with me. You know I love the job. You love the job. So why, oh why, does our primero numero uno boss love to mess with us? Is it just fun for him?"

"Honestly? Yeah. I think he loves it," Chaundra laughed. "What's happening?"

"What's happening is this new "side quest,"" Rachael said, making air quotes. "Peter and I now have to spend even more time together to build up our clientele and scout locations. This recognition would be fantastic if I didn't have to spend all of my time with Peter. Yech!"

Chaundra raised her eyebrows. "He's making the two of you work together outside of the team-building? Wow. I really feel for you. I don't know how you can stand being around him as much as you already are. After the way he messed with Casey..." Chaundra just shook her head and trailed off. "So what are you going to do?"

"What can I do? I'm going to work with Peter. Maybe it won't be so bad. He'll just have to get over himself."

"Facts. Don't let him get to you. Call me if you need to let off some steam. I've got you." Chaundra wheeled her chair back into her cubicle and answered her ringing phone.

Rachael threw up a peace hand sign and returned to her desk as well. Maybe it wouldn't be so bad, she thought. She just had to parlay the activities into a career-making experience. The one thing she was glad about was that she was not Peter's type. There was no reason for her to end up on the receiving end of his advances. Years of dating, or rather lack of dating, had clearly informed Rachael that she was not "that girl." Her confidence was too strong, her style too outrageous, her wit too quick and sharp to be the girl that every guy made a play for. She liked to think of it as her superpower. It saved her from a lot of jerks and a lot of negative experiences. There was no way she wanted to go through the nonsense that her girlfriends, Chaundra included, had experienced. Rachael was fine being an independent black woman. What was the old saying? You can do bad all by yourself? Better to be on her own than caught up with a no-good man.

Rachael took a sip of her coffee and settled into the day's tasks. She was just starting to relax when an instant message came through.

Insta-chat Kane: Little Bird

Insta-chat Palmer: *angry face emoji*

Insta-chat Kane: Lol. Sorry, LB. Looks like we have a new project together. Meet me in my office, and we can discuss plans.

Insta-chat Palmer: No, thank you. We've seen enough of each other today.

Insta-chat Kane: You're not going to be able to avoid me forever.

Insta-chat Palmer: But I can avoid you as long as possible. Today is not your day.

Insta-chat Kane: Don't worry, it will be soon enough, LB. *wink emoji*

Rachael knew this was going to happen. Peter was going to take full advantage of this pairing and annoy the hell out of her. She toyed with blocking him on the insta-chat for a moment but thought better of it. Peter was an executive, after all. She wasn't sure if he was also the vindictive type.

Insta-chat Palmer: Until then, let's keep things to a minimum. We can talk when we get our first assignment. I wouldn't want to waste all of the excitement that comes from being around you. Have the day you deserve!

Chapter Five

RODRIGO'S BAR AND GRILLE

Peter pulled his sleek, matte, black-on-black Rivian R1S into the parking lot of Rodrigo's Bar and Grille. Had he known he was going to have to meet his father after work, he would never have driven his baby to work. The SUV was his pride and joy and a luxurious splurge. Unfortunately, the lux vehicle was only going to fuel his father's belief that he had money to spare. Evan Kane had no shame in depending heavily on his oldest child to support him financially. It started fairly early in Peter's life. As soon as Peter was old enough to get an after-school job, Evan started pocketing money under the guise of teaching his son how to be an adult- pay a small amount for rent and put a small amount toward utilities. Want a cell phone with extra gigs and minutes? Peter could pay for that, too. Evan had hinted that all the money would be set aside for Peter's college years. Pay a little now, and his dad would be saving the money in an account for him. All the money being collected was merely an exercise, not actually being put to use. Fast forward to Peter's freshman year of college, and the money was nowhere to be found. Evan had entangled himself with his second wife, and of course, she was pregnant with Peter's future little sister, Emma. So began Peter's life as supplemental income to his dad.

Evan was waiting for him. His black hair, only slightly greying at the temples, fell foppishly across his brow. His sapphire blue eyes which mirrored Peter's, sparkled at the sight of his son. Clad in black denim and a blazer-cut leather jacket, Evan gave the appearance of a man who was well-off, confident, and extremely handsome. His mouth quirked into a charming grin.

"Come here and give your pop a hug!" Evan said warmly as he approached Peter's vehicle. Peter had barely shut the SUV door before he was pulled into an overwhelming bear hug.

"Hi, Dad," Peter said. Reluctantly, Peter sunk into the embrace, enjoying the temporary familial sensations. He hated to admit how much he needed it.

"Well, let's go inside. I want to hear about your day and that new SUV. How much did something like that set you back?"

The two men headed into the restaurant. One felt hopeful and excited, while the younger man felt nothing but dread at the prospect of an evening spent with the man who used to be his hero.

Once inside the restaurant, they were seated at a corner table away from the door. Their server, a buxom redhead in her late thirties, came over to the table to take their order.

"Gentleman, can I take your drinks order, or would you like to here the specials?" she asked with a smile as she took in the two handsome men.

"If they're as special as you, I'd love to hear them," Evan flattered, flashing her a thousand-watt smile and looking her directly in the eye. "What's your name? You're lovely."

Inwardly, Peter groaned. Evan couldn't be around a pretty woman without attempting the charm.

"Barbara," the waitress said as a rosy glow heightened the color of her cheeks. She began to prattle off the specials as Evan focused his attention soley on the waitress. His smile grew as she went on.

"Well, that all sounds delicious! Especially when you describe it. I think I'll have that special, darlin'."

"And for you?" Barbara asked Peter.

"Just an old-fashioned and some fries, thank you. We have important business to discuss." Peter said dismissively.

He didn't want to be rude to the woman, but he had no desire to watch his father flirt, let alone begin another relationship. For all he knew, Barabar might end up being wife number five. If he could curb that from happening, then he would do his best. The server walked away with their order, only turning slightly to glance over her shoulder and give Evan a grin.

"Dad, why do you have to do that all the time? "

"What? I was just being friendly."

"Well, quit it. Friendly for you always leads to three things- a divorce, a wedding, and a baby. And not usually in that order. You have enough on your plate, so can you just not?"

"Whatever, kid. So, do you have the money? I don't want to let Emma down."

Peter ran his fingers through his hair and stared at the table. Where was that drink? He could really use it right now.

"You're worried about letting Emma down? Don't promise what you can't follow through on."

"Listen, fruit of my loins, you're the one working right now. You can do this for me. It's not like I didn't do right by you when you were a kid. It's not going to hurt for you to pay back a little of what you owe."

"What do you mean 'what I owe'?"

"Nevermind. It was a bad choice of words."

The drinks arrived in time to cut off Peter's reply. He didn't want to make a scene in this restaurant.

Peter picked up his drink and took a long pull of the brown liquor.

"Listen, Dad. You know that I love my sisters, and I want the best for them. That includes wanting to see *you* give them your best. If that means that you don't make promises you can't follow through on, then that's what you do. You can't fall back on me to be the answer all of the time."

"Fall back on you? Fall back on you? Boy, I think you better get one thing straight." Evan leaned forward over the table, eyes narrowed. "I'm not falling back on you. This is the least that you can do. You know I had prospects before you came along. I was making something of myself and then your mother fell pregnant with you. *Helping* me out once in a while is the least you can do. I changed my whole life's trajectory to keep you in diapers, to get you into good schools. All of that just for you to give me your ass to kiss right now? You've got the money, Mr. Shiny SUV. I know how much one of those things costs. Unbelievable."

Peter had heard some variation of this before. Every time he attempted to get his father to step up and be better, out came the defensive words and the guilt that he lay at Peter's feet for existing. Frustration and irritation infused his next words.

"Fine. I fucked up your life being born. It's nothing I haven't heard before. I'm not even here to argue with you. Just be better, man. Don't blow sunshine at my sisters. Give them something real, something that comes from you. I can deal with this nonsense, but they shouldn't have to."

"Oh, you're tired of hearing about my sacrifice? It's too much to give your dad a few dollars to help out your sisters. You know, I was about to make it big as an actor. I gave up a major role, what would have been my breakthrough role to start a regular job to take care of you."

Evan paused as Barbara, the waitress, returned to the table with his lobster-topped filet mignon, dauphinoise potatoes, and roasted asparagus.

"Thank you, darling. This looks amazing. My compliments to you and the chef."

Barbara blushed and nodded as she walked away. Peter just shook his head and shoved more fries into his mouth.

"Alright, kid, I came here to have a nice meal with you. You've busted my chops and said what you had to say. I get it. Let's play nice. We're in this restaurant, we've got beautiful food, gorgeous eye candy. I think that's enough for one evening. Emma's going to be ecstatic. How about that?"

"I'm happy I can help Emma. She's going places," Peter said, deciding he made enough points for one night. Hopefully, his dad would actually take it all to heart.

The energy shifted for the remainder of the meal. Peter watched his dad devour the most expensive meal on the menu while he sipped his old-fashioned and nibbled on French fries. He came to terms with the fact that Evan was always, first and foremost, going to be Evan.

Chapter Six

SHOPPING WITH MIMI PALMER

"Thank you for picking me up, baby." MiMi said as Rachael helped her down the recently installed ramp at her grandparent's front door.

"It's no problem, MiMi. You call me whenever you need me," Rachael assured.

"You take such good care of us. Your Pops and I truly appreciate you," MiMi gushed as she stopped to give her granddaughter a kiss on the cheek. "Now enough of that, let's get shopping! CHARGE!!!"

Rachael laughed as she helped get MiMi situated in the front seat of the car. "Where do you want to go first? The outlets or the pharmacy? I don't want you burning a hole in that card too fast."

"Let's go to the pharmacy and get that boring stuff over with. Then I can enjoy my dessert, shopping for the fun stuff."

They rode in companionable silence for several minutes before MiMi glanced over at Rachael and frowned.

"What is it MiMi?" Rachael asked.

"You haven't mentioned your asshole. You didn't take my advice this week, did you?"

"No, and I'm not going to speak to him unless I have to. How can you tell I didn't talk to him?"

"You've got that pinched, dried up look. Like you licked an unripe persimmon. Your eyes are squinty, and your mouths puckered."

"Gee, thanks, MiMi. I thought I looked pretty good today. Way to build a girl's confidence."

"I'm not tryin' to knock you. I just can tell your cogs have yet to be greased. You need oiling, baby girl!"

"Hmmph! Not from that man I don't."

Rachael pulled into the lot and parked the car. Once they were inside the drugstore, Rachael went to the prescription counter while MiMi wandered the aisles looking for clearance items and various other items she didn't really need. She couldn't believe her grandmother was trying to push her towards a man that she only knew him as The Asshole. If she only knew him, she would loathe him, too. Everything about Peter made Rachael's skin itch. The way he flirted with every woman at the job, his over-confidence. Seriously, who just calls Mr. Pfeiffer "Hendrick"? No one else ever simply called him Hendrick. The CEO's whole demeanor seemed to demand the "Mr." Only Peter Kane would be so bold and comfortable. Then there was the way he was always smiling and twinkling at her, specifically. It wasn't lost on Rachael that for the last several team-building outings, Peter focused almost exclusively on her with his flirtation. Sure, he would do the obligatory flirt or comment with any other woman around but he always seemed to return back to her with laser focus and more intense stares. Plus, he was selfish. She only had to look at how he used Casey's ex-fiance, Kerry Dennis. Only an asshole would seduce a woman away from her perfectly handsome fiancé and then drop her when she seemed completely into him. Peter was that asshole. She just couldn't humor her grandmother on this one. What would she look like pursuing a man like that? Not to mention, he held a higher position in the company. People would swear up and down that she was trying to sleep her way up the corporate ladder. Nope, there was no way she was trying to get with him... even if he did have pretty eyes.

"I wish I would give that man the time of..." Rachael was mumbling to herself when her eyes fell on a sight she never could have prepared for.

MiMi was standing in the As Seen on TV aisle talking to a man. A man who was earnestly paying attention to her every word as she espoused the wonders of some random kitchen gadget. He was standing with his back to her. He stood about 6'3', broad shoulders filled out a slightly worn t-shirt from a rock band, dark washed jeans hugging his legs in all of the right ways- not too tight, not too loose. Black wavy hair peaked out from under his baseball cap and brushed against the color of his shirt. Rachael stood just out of MiMi's line of site and listened in. From the back, this was the type of man that Rachael could be interested in. She was a sucker for a nice set of broad shoulders. They just looked capable. This guy also had well-muscled arms that didn't look too bulky but definitely would be strong enough to pick her up and hold her tight. This is exactly the type of guy she wished her grandmother would consider, not her jackass work colleague. Any man who was willing to listen to her grandmother talk about frivolous gadgets was okay in her book.

"This fancy potato peeler is going to do wonders for me in the kitchen, let me tell you! See, I cook with my granddaughter every Wednesday night. She does all of the chopping and peeling for me 'cause the arthritis just doesn't let me move the way I used to, you know?"

The man nodded his head in acknowledgment.

"We make delicious, home-cooked meals. Have you had a home-cooked meal lately?" MiMi continued, not giving the man a chance to reply. "My gorgeous grandbaby can really cook. Would you mind getting me that mint green peeler on the top shelf? I can't reach it. Anyway, she's single. Are you single?"

As he reached for the potato peeler, the hem of his T-shirt rose up, revealing the dark golden tanned skin of a well-sculpted back. *Yes, please! Go MiMi!* Rachael thought as she watched from her hidden vantage point. At the sound of his chuckled response, Rachael felt a chill run through her veins. It couldn't be— there's no way.... She closed her eyes, hoping that her ears had deceived her.

"I am single. I bet you both make a wonderful dinner."

Rachae's ears proved her hopes wrong. She knew exactly who this man was.

"Oh, we sure do. I've taught her everything I know. It's kept my husband coming back for seconds and thirds for the last fifty-five years! She could do the same for... the right handsome man."

Rachael could hear the flirtation in her grandmother's voice, attempting to entice the man.

"You should join us one Wednesday evening for dinner!" MiMi said as if it had just occurred to her. "Give me your number, and I'll let you know when you should join us."

As far as pickup artists go, MiMi seemed to run the game. She had his phone in her hand as fast as lightning. "I'll just text myself with your phone. You don't mind, do you? Mmmhmmm... There you go. I'm all set. Actually, you should meet my girl. She's around here somewhere."

Rachael gasped and started to speed-walk away from the aisle that her grandmother was in. The faster she got away, the better. She looked for the biggest floor display she could find and hoped it would be enough to hide her from her grandmother and that... that man! Ugh.... How is it possible that the one man that MiMi would find would be the same man who got under her skin on a daily basis?

"What did you say your name was again? I need to be sure to enter you in my phone correctly. My husband would have a fit seeing me text Drugstore Hottie." MiMi and the man both laughed.

"My name is Peter, Peter Kane, in case you want to look me up online and make sure I'm safe."

That was all the confirmation Rachael needed to hear. There was no doubt that she was a magnet for the worst things. She only hoped they wouldn't find her.

"Thank you, Peter. Let's go find my grandbaby. Rachael! Where are you?" MiMi called. "I have a treat for you."

"You're quite the little matchmaker, aren't you?" Peter laughed. "I've never heard myself referred to as a treat for someone's granddaughter before."

Rachael could hear their voices getting closer and cringed inwardly. As they approached, she grabbed the largest box she could find and held it up over her face. She hoped to look like a customer who was deeply contemplating the contents of the package.

"Oh, there you are! I know you had to have heard me calling for you." MiMi's voice was almost in front of her. "Why didn't you answer me? I want to introduce you to someone. Why are you hiding behind this stack of pads?"

"Hi, MiMi," Rachael faltered. "Sorry, I was just really excited to find this product. I've been looking for it for a while." She still held the box over her face.

"Come on, girl, put that box of Extra Heavy Flow Overnight Pads down. I have someone I want you to meet. He's going to be joining us for dinner one night soon."

Rachael slowly lowered the box and stepped from behind the Period Pyramid display of all things menstrual.

"Peter," MiMi said as she held Rachael's hand and pulled her forward so he could get a good look at her, "I'd like you to meet my granddaughter, Rachael. Isn't she beautiful?"

Peter's smile was almost wider than his face somehow as he looked at Rachael. The laughter in his eyes was almost more than Rachael could take, and she started to pull away, but MiMi only gripped her tighter.

"My goodness! She sure is, but then, with you as her grandmother, how could she be anything but beautiful? I can't wait to come over for dinner!"

Peter looked at Rachael and gave her a knowing smile.

"Well, that's just great," Rachael quipped, giving Peter an icy smile. "MiMi we really need to get going if we're going to get all of our errands in before Pops gets dropped off from his club."

"Oh, you're right! Sorry to rush away, but I'll be in touch. Look for my text, Peter!" MiMi said as they bustled off to the checkout.

"Looking forward to it! Have a wonderful day! And Rachael, it was *really* good to see you."

Of course Peter had to have the last word, Rachael thought.

* * *

Rachael sat quietly in the car, listening to MiMi's excitement about the nice, handsome man she had met at the drug store. If she had to hear one more word about how her grandmother thought Peter was just perfect for her, she would scream. Instead, she just gave a low growl.

"What are you making those noises for, baby? I know you had to find him handsome."

"MiMi... you know how I've been telling you about the man I work with?"

"The asshole? Yes."

"He's the asshole. Peter Kane is the asshole! I don't want to have dinner with him EVER. It's bad enough I have to see him at work. We're literally stuck together, even after hours. Our boss has given us an additional side project. We have to spend even more time together."

"Really? He seemed nice to me. So you two have to see each other for work outside of business hours?" MiMi glanced over at Rachael and grinned. "Hmm.... I think you're just reading him wrong."

"I'm seriously not. Didn't you just feel the sleaze roll off of him?"

"Nope! I saw a good-looking, muscley hunk of a man. Shoot, if your grandfather wasn't the most amazing man ever, I would consider turning into an old THOT for Peter."

Rachael groaned again. This was all just so cringe for her.

"Mimi, that is so gross."

"Why? I am old enough and wise enough to know that one wrinkle doesn't stop the show. I know a fun ride when I see one."

"Okay, that's more than enough. I really don't want to talk about you THOTing out or about Peter. I'll see him plenty in the future. So please don't invite him to dinner this week."

"Okay, I'll leave it be. I won't invite him over this week."

Rachael gave a sigh of relief. Once she dropped Mimi off and she was alone in her car, she had time to rehash the disastrous pharmacy trip. Unfortunately, the only parts that kept replaying in her mind were the flex of Peter's arm as he reached up for the peeler and that little glimpse of his golden skin and firm torso. The charming flash of mirth in his eyes, when he saw her hiding behind the box of pads, followed her all the way home.

To: Kane, Peter; Palmer, Rachael

From: Kathy Starnes (on behalf of Hendrick Pfeiffer, CEO)

Subject: Leadership Jam-Side Project Event #1

Dear Colleagues,

The time has come for your first outing. You will be meeting Pedro Cartagena this Thursday evening at Hotel Brasilia. He is a potential client from Honduras. I would like for you to both show him a great time and get him used to the idea of partnering with WCP Industries to set up a new paper manufacturing site. We want it to be sustainable, profitable, and beneficial to the workers in his country. By extolling the virtues of our company and showing him a good time, we can achieve success.

In addition, you both will learn just how valuable your teamwork is. Remember, we're better together, and togetherness is what we are all about at WCP. This should be a match made in heaven.

Please have a report prepared and delivered by the following Monday morning for my review.

Sincerely,

Hendrick Pfeiffer, CEO

* * *

Insta-chat Kane: Little Bird

Insta-chat Palmer: *angry emoji*

Insta-chat Kane: Why so angry? Your grandmother is a delightful lady.

Insta-chat Palmer: She's lovely. Forget you ever met her.

Insta-chat Kane: She's unforgettable.

Insta-chat Palmer: Why are you bothering me? If it's not work-related you can leave me in peace.

Insta-chat Kane: Actually, it is work-related. I will pick you up at 6:00 P.M. so we can prepare for our meeting with Mr. Cartagena. What is your address?

Insta-chat Palmer: This is not a date. You do not need my address.

Insta-chat Kane: Fine. Meet me here and we will ride over to the restaurant together so we can strategize and recap. Does that meet your approval? Or would you rather show up wind-blown from your scooter?

Insta-chat Palmer: 6:00 P.M. at the front door of the building. And I always look amazing when I get off my scooter.

Insta-chat Kane: You do always look amazing

Insta-chat Palmer: *eyeroll emoji*

End of chat

Chapter Seven

"Chaundra, I can't believe Mr. Pfeiffer is making me do this," Rachael said as the two women stood in front of the large mirror in the first-floor women's room.

"I've been thinking about Mr. Pfeiffer, and I've got to say he has the strangest way of building team camaraderie. Anyone can see how much you loathe being around Peter," Chaundra surmised.

"Right? I honestly could just scream, but you know what? I won't give Peter the satisfaction." Rachael pulled her freshly touched-up electric blue and purple hair from its high-top bun, letting it flow down the left side of her face and shoulder in waterfall-like waves. "I'm going to dazzle Mr. Pedro Cartagena in spite of Peter. If this goes off without a hitch, maybe this will be the last side quest I have to go on."

"That's right!" Chaundra turned to Rachael and gave her a hug. "Here's to one and done!"

"I guess I better go meet the he-demon and get this over with."

Rachael left the restroom and headed for the front entrance. Peter was waiting for her, leaning against his Rivian. His dark waves were brushed back and away from his face, curling slightly around his ears. His beard was freshly shaven, and the sharp lines highlighted his strong, chiseled jaw and angular cheekbones. *Ugh... what is with this man? Why does he always look like he's advertising something high-end?* Rachael thought.

"Rachael," Peter called, pulling away from the side of his vehicle. "Right on time, like I knew you would be. Are you ready to go?"

"Yes, let's do this thing," Rachael answered and walked toward the open door of the SUV.

"You look wonderful. Your hair looks amazing," Peter whispered as he placed his hand on the small of her back to help her into the vehicle.

"Peter! Peter!" a female voice called out just as Rachael was fully seated.

Rachael saw Peter's face tense at the sound of the voice. She glanced over his shoulder and saw a flash of blonde hair as arms wrapped around Peter.

"Where have you been? I've been trying to reach you for so long. I miss you!"

"Kerry," Peter said, untangling from the woman's grasp. "I'm busy. There's a reason I haven't returned your calls. We ended things. I know you remember. Everyone at WCP remembers."

"I just miss you so much. We really should get together for coffee or something," Kerry said, ignoring everything Peter said.

Rachael watched as Peter's shoulders tensed. She noticed the way his eyes crinkled in frustration and even noted a bit of panic. Against her better judgment, she felt compelled to help extract him from the moment. Besides, even though he was a womanizer, Kerry was the one who actually destroyed a relationship. Peter was only the tool. She had no sympathy for the clearly desperate and thirsty woman.

"Peter, we really need to get going. We have reservations and guests waiting," Rachael interrupted. This was just too much. She did not have time to watch his soap opera of a life play out in front of her.

Kerry pushed her head past Peter's shoulder and looked Rachael up and down with a curled lip.

"Peter. Why are you with this woman?" Kerry's tone was pure disgust.

"Excuse me?" Rachael spoke before Peter could. "You can address me if you want to know who I am. You clearly see me. Show me some respect even if you can't show it to yourself."

"You are NOT seeing her. We had something good. We still can," Kerry purred to Peter.

"Kerry." Peter had a warning tone to his voice. "Just go back inside and leave me alone. We don't have time for whatever this is."

Peter closed Rachael's door, giving Kerry his back, and walked to the driver's side. He shook his head and gave Rachael an apologetic smile as he started the engine. Rachael just gave him a look of pure irritation and rolled the window down to get a little air.

"You're just another office trick! Don't get used to him," Kerry yelled as Peter put the car in drive. "He'll come right back to me!"

The tension in the car was thick. Peter appeared clearly uncomfortable. He stared straight ahead, glancing at Rachael occasionally from the corner of his eye. She kept her face turned away from him and stared out the window, then she fidgeted with her bag, opening it and taking inventory of the contents. When her silence became too loud, she turned on the stereo and was pleasantly surprised to hear gentle lo-fi music. Her shoulders relaxed a bit, and she allowed her head to rest against the seat.

"At least your taste in music is pleasant," Rachael said quietly.

"Rachael, I- I want to apologize."

"You don't have to apologize to me. I'm not your woman."

"I know, but you still shouldn't have had to deal with any of that."

"Listen, no offense, but we both know you've spent most of your time here at WCP as a man-whore. Pardon the expression. I don't care. You do you."

Peter let out a frustrated breath of air.

"Do you have to be so prickly? I'm trying to apologize. Look, I know that my actions have not painted me in the best light over the last few years, but I'm not the villain that I appear to be."

"Oh really? So, you're not the man that I watched taunt my friend about stealing his fiancé? That wasn't you fighting Casey at the last formal team-building exercise?"

"Okay." Peter shook his head. "I may have done those things, but I also got the point. I fucked around, and I found out. I *can* learn from my mistakes. I'm not that guy anymore. I even felt bad about how all of that went down once I thought about it."

"Have you apologized? Unless you actually take action to repair what you've damaged, then all of the feeling bad in the world doesn't amount to anything."

"No," Peter shook his head. "What would I even say to the guy? Most people don't want to hear, 'Hey, man. I'm sorry I slept with your fiancé and made you the laughingstock of the company."

"You ass! Why would you even think that's what I mean?" Rachael laughed despite herself. It wasn't funny, really, but the idea of Peter walking up to Casey and saying that cracked her up. She was fairly certain he'd come back with a sore jaw. She kind of liked the idea.

"No, don't tell him you're sorry. Show that you're sorry with your actions. Learn what makes you tick. Why do you do the things you do? Have some real self-actualization and growth. If you do that, things are going to change for you. You'll get control over yourself and your life. Because right now, the way you live, as far as what I've seen around the office... Man, you're out of control. I don't know what you're looking for or whose approval you need, but the way you're going about things at work, ain't it."

"Thanks for the armchair analysis." Peter bristled at her words. "Let's have a bit more music and a lot less talk."

He turned the volume up and drove for several more miles, ruminating or perhaps stewing over her words. *Whatever.* Rachael thought. *He can stay pissed for all I care. Someone had to tell him.*

Chapter Eight

MEETING SEÑOR PEDRO CARTAGENA

Peter and Rachael arrived at Hotel Brasilia twenty minutes early. Peter hated to be late and had originally seen it as an opportunity to share some alone time with Rachael. He thought Bess, Rachael's grandmother, was on to something. It wouldn't hurt to get to know Rachael a little better. He's already acknowledged that she was someone that he could get a bit more serious about. He just didn't know how to go about it. Unfortunately, after the tense words of the ride to the restaurant, he had the distinct feeling that Rachael despised him.

"We have reservations for Peter Kane," Peter said to the maître d'.

"Right this way. The other members of your party have already arrived."

Rachael glanced over at Peter, eyebrows raised.

"I thought you said we were getting here early?" Rachael whispered.

"We are. The reservations are for 7:15," Peter replied.

"I guess we're not the only ones to adhere to the idea of being late if you're on time. Now's the time to put on your charm. We don't know how long Mr. Cartagena has been waiting. Best foot forward!"

Peter put on his most charming smile and followed the maître d' to the table. His bluster and confidence faltered as he noted that Mr. Cartagena was not alone at the table.

"Peter, Rachael. It's good to see you both." The firm, no-nonsense voice of Kathy Starnes, assistant to Mr. Hendrick Pfeiffer, greeted them. "Let me introduce you to our esteemed guest, Señor Pedro Cartagena."

Kathy gestured to a handsome man to her left. Pedro Cartagena nodded at Peter. Turning to Rachael, he turned up the wattage on his smile.

On Kathy's right sat Mr. Pfeiffer.

"Pedro, Peter and Rachael are rising stars here at WCP. I wanted to be sure to bring out our brightest stars to meet you and celebrate your visit," Hendrick said.

Realizing that they were both standing stupidly by, saying nothing, Peter stepped forward and offered his hand. Bouncing back from his surprise at seeing his boss with full confidence.

"Mr. Cartagena, it is a pleasure for Rachael and I to meet you. My apologies for having you wait for us to arrive. Our intent was to be here to welcome you at your arrival." Peter said.

"It's a pleasure to meet you. Hendrick, Kathy, and I decided to arrive early and catch up on old times." Pedro said in a deep, smooth, accented voice. "Please, sit down and join us. I have heard a lot about you two. I'm looking forward to getting to know you both better."

Peter pulled out a seat at the table for Rachael before taking his own seat next to her. Glancing around the table, six sets of eyes stared back at them. Mr. Pfeiffer's mirth-filled eyes danced in the candlelight. Kathy looked both aloof and alert, a seeming contradiction that she mastered. Señor Cartagena's eyes held a curious but knowing look.

"Mr. Cartagena, it is so good to be here with you this evening. How long will you be staying with us? I'd love to show you more of our beautiful city," Rachael offered.

"I will be here for about a week, more if business goes well. I would love to see more," he responded.

"That's wonderful," Peter jumped in before Rachael could respond. Rachael smiled politely but gave Peter the side-eye.

"Anyway," Rachael jumped back into the conversation. "There are some beautiful botanical gardens that I would love to take you to. They may pale in comparison to the tropical blooms in your local area of Honduras, but I think you will enjoy them all the same."

"I see you have done your research. I would love to see them, but I thought I would be working with the both of you?"

"Indeed, you will," Mr. Pfeiffer interjected. "Rachael and Peter have a very unique chemistry. You will get the most benefit by working with the two of them together."

It was Peter's turn to give Rachael a pointed look. *Does she want us to lose this opportunity?* Peter thought.

"Of course, I did not mean to imply that Peter would not be joining us. We work great as a team, don't we, Peter?" Rachael corrected.

"Absolutely," Peter said.

"Well, enough about business. Let's enjoy this wonderful meal."

They went on to have a robust and delicious meal pre-ordered by Mr. Pfieffer. Once the dinner was over, the initial tension that Peter and Rachael had felt from the drive over had finally faded. The presence of their CEO had completely put Peter off of his usual game. He prided himself on always being ready and able to charm anyone. He wanted to get back on good footing with Mr. Cartagena. Without being able to speak privately with Rachael, he felt off-balance. They needed to get back on the same page to present a strong and cohesive force, especially since their performance was able to be judged firsthand by Hendrick and Kathy.

"Did you know that this restaurant has an upper floor with dancing and live music?" Peter asked.

Mr. Cartagena's eyes lit up.

"I would love to dance. We have had enough of business for the night. Let us get up and move our bodies with joy!" Pedro said.

"Splendid idea! What a great way to see you move as one on the dance floor," Mr. Pfeiffer added.

"I would love to dance as well, Peter," Kathy said. "I can't resist the call of the beat."

Chapter Nine

DANCE LIKE NO ONE IS WATCHING

Hotel Brasilia's nightclub was jumping. The vibe was a mix of Caribbean, Bachata, Samba, and Afrobeats. Couples shimmied and wiggled their hips in time to the music with the complicated footwork of the southern hemisphere. Large hand drums and palm trees decorated the walls of the club. It was crowded, but with Mr. Pfeiffer's credentials, the group was whisked off to the VIP section above the main dance floor. Bottle service was brought to their table by a beautiful young woman. She smiled at all in attendance but made a point bending forward a little more deeply when it came to pouring Peter's drink, assuring that her ample cleavage was in his line of sight for as long as possible. Peter smirked at the young woman. He knew exactly what she was doing. Rachael rolled her eyes. This was par for the course. She had to admit, begrudgingly, that as handsome as he was, and he looked particularly good tonight, women were going to show their interest. Once all of the drinks were poured and the server left the table alone, Mr. Cartagena cleared his throat.

"Ms. Rachael, you look lovely tonight would you care to join me on the dancefloor?"

"I would love to," Rachel answered as she took his extended hand. She hoped he would be a skilled dancer.

"I hope you do not mind if I borrow your lady for a moment," Pedro hinted to Peter.

"Oh, not at all," Peter said. "She's all yours." He waved them on with a shooing motion.

Rachael found herself on the dance floor with the extremely handsome mogul. His arm encircled her waist firmly as they danced to a popular bachata. Rachael got lost in the beat as he led her around the floor, guiding her hips in a fluid motion. She enjoyed the chance to shake off thoughts of being forced to work with Peter. Her mind felt free for the first time in quite a while, which is why her steps faltered with Señor Cartagena's words.

"Ah, young love. What I would give to be in Peter's shoes. Having the love of a beautiful woman such as yourself."

"Wait. What? No, no. Peter and I are *not* together," Rachael declared, trying to catch the rhythm.

"No? Hmmm." Pedro took this opportunity to spin her out and back in, pulling her close to his body and swiveling their bodies together. "So he doesn't mind that I dance with you this closely?"

Mr. Cartagena kept their bodies flush and began to repeat the same hip-shaking moves from before, but this time, they did not feel as business-like. "I am not so sure. I think he will not be in as jovial of a mood when we return. You wait and see."

"Señor Cartagena," Rachael started.

"Call me Pedro, and if you don't mind, may I call you Raquel?"

"Sure. Pedro, Peter loves all women in the same way that a dog loves every new bone their way. We are not compatible. Above all else, I am not interested."

"Raquel, Raquel," Pedro brought his hands to both sides of her head and brought them down, outlining her entire frame without actually touching her. "Can I tell you a secret?"

Rachael nodded.

"I see you, and I know that you and Peter— muy lindo! You will be beautiful together."

Once again, Pedro spun Rachael away and brought her back.

Rachael started to protest but was hushed by a caress to the cheek. "Love, amor. This is life's essence, and it only burns brighter when there is passion and friction. I feel this deeply in you and Peter. Trust me, cara mia. You will see."

Rachael was torn between objecting to his words and placating him. He was a potential special client, and he needed to be pleased. She weighed all of her options, pleasing Hendrick, the potential for employment advancement vs destroying millions of dollars in revenue, and a potential new site. She would keep her mouth shut for the time being and ride this out.

"You are skeptical, but look," Pedro pointed up to the VIP section. Peter's eyes were glued to the two of them as they danced, and his face held a look of fierce indignation, and though she doubted it, there was a sense of possessiveness that she felt was unwarranted. Damn, she didn't want to admit it, but she felt her heart flutter and shiver up her spine. "Ah... you see it, too. I can tell. Let's give him something to latch on to before we head back."

With those words, he pulled her into a tight embrace, his nose and lips coming close to grazing her neck and using his hips to practically grind into her with seductive movements. Rachael wanted to push back, but before she even had the chance, she heard Peter's voice pierce through the Latin rhythms and a hand fall upon her shoulder.

"Señor Cartagena, Kathy would like to dance. Let me relieve you of your partner. I need a word with Rachael for a moment," Peter said sharply, edged but cloaked in politeness.

"I would love to dance with Kathy. Remember what I said, Raquel, cara mia. Passion and fire!"

"We'll see, Pedro," Rachael countered.

Chapter Ten

PREVIOUSLY IN THE VIP SECTION

Hendrick Pfeiffer watched as Rachael and Señor Cartagena exited the VIP section, then turned his gaze back to Peter and smiled.

"Peter, how are things going between you and Ms. Palmer? I hope you both have worked out whatever little spat you had in the elevator. Has she learned your worth?" Hendrick asked.

Peter leaned back in his club chair, resting his head in his hands, aping the look of the extremely relaxed CEO. "I like to think so," he surmised.

"Very good," Hendrick said.

"Are you certain? I thought I felt a distinct lack of cohesiveness when you first arrived," Kathy spoke up. Peter winced at the recognition of their lackluster entrance. He had forgotten Kathy was there; she sat so ramrod straight and silent. As Mr. Pfeiffer's assistant in all matters, it was her job to observe silently and pick up on the things that Hendrick might miss. She was extremely good at her job.

"We may have had a slight hiccup on the way over, but it was so minor. Nothing that couldn't be danced away." Peter threw a dazzling smile at Kathy, hoping to distract her with his good looks. He knew he could lead just about any woman off their topic with a smoldering look or well-placed smile.

"No need to flirt with me, Mr. Kane," Kathy asserted. "I am immune to such foolishness. I'm not one of the young ladies at the office, and neither is Ms. Palmer. You'll have to work much harder if you want to achieve your goals. You'll need to start being real."

Peter had enough sense to look mildly abashed. Hendrick broke out into peals of laughter.

"Ah, don't worry, my boy. I'm rooting for you both," Hendrick said. "I have been observing you for a long time. I believe you have exactly what the other needs to make you complete—a complete team. I haven't failed yet, and I don't intend to start."

"He's right, you know," Kathy's piercing voice cut through the music. "Mr. Pfeiffer has yet to be wrong in his pairings. Build the team, and the team will build the harmony you seek."

Peter looked at them and picked up his drink. "Indeed. Cryptic, but I like it."

Hendrick giggled again. "Not so very cryptic. Let's see how your teammate is doing with our future business partner."

Peter looked down on the dance floor and frowned. He watched as Señor Cartagena whirled and twirled Rachael across the floor. They were dancing awfully close, too close for his taste. He watched as they practically began to dirty dance on beat. He heard a slight, rumbling growl and realized it was coming from himself. He cleared his throat and started to look away.

"They do look good together. Who knows, maybe this will lead to more than just a business merger. Maybe... we're watching the beginnings of an epic love affair," Kathy goaded.

Peter turned and looked at her briefly. He fought to hold back the sneer that threatened to pass his lips.

"I do think you're right. They look wonderful together!" Mr. Pfeiffer added.

Peter brought his eyes back to the spectacle on the floor. The man could dance, and he was taking full advantage of his skill to put the moves on Rachael. Peter felt it viscerally. He rejected the sight before him. Rachael would *not* belong to that man. She needed someone like him. Just as the thought entered his mind, Rachael made eye contact with him. They held the gaze for a beat longer than necessary. Señor Cartagena brought her back to his attention and looked as though he meant to kiss her. Before he could stop himself, Peter was on his feet and heading down to the dance floor.

"Remember, Peter, I don't have a policy against dating your coworker!" Hendrick called out to Peter, and then collapsed onto Kathy's stalwart shoulder in a fit of giggles and laughter. That giggle was the last thing Peter heard as he made his way down the steps to the dance floor.

Chapter Eleven

RHYTHM OF THE NIGHT

Peter frowned and wrapped his arm around her waist as the music switched to Afrobeats. The upbeat and sensual grooves of the music punctuated the moment that Señor Pedro Cartagena went back to the VIP section to find Kathy.

"Was he upsetting you?" Peter asked. "I don't want to see you being taken advantage of. I know that this deal is important to WCP, but no one should be taking liberties with you."

Rachael raised an eyebrow at him. "Are you concerned? You don't need to worry about me. I can take care of myself."

"I know you can, but that doesn't mean I can't still be concerned about you. I'm always going to offer my assistance if I see someone in an uncomfortable situation. Especially you," Peter proclaimed.

"Especially me?" Rachael asked, a doubtful expression on her face.

"Yes, we're partners. I wouldn't leave my partner in the lurch."

Peter's hips swayed expertly to the music as he held Rachael close. Rachael smiled up at him, a genuine smile despite the cutting words that next left her lips.

"I didn't think you knew what loyalty was. It certainly hasn't been your strong suit at the office. Ask Kerry."

Peter gave a mental groan as he turned Rachael out and in front of him. They started doing a popular dance routine to Burna Boy's *On the Low*. With each step and wind of their bodies, Peter and Rachael got closer. The dancing was so intense and focused that Peter didn't have a breath to give her a response. The music gradually transitioned into a slower, more sensual beat, and Peter was able to once again bring Rachael back into his arms.

"I see you've got moves. I'm impressed," Rachael admitted as she rested a hand on his chest. Instinctively, Peter rested his hand on top of hers, holding her there. It was a mirror of the position that Hendrick found them in on the elevator, only this time, their bodies moved in tandem to the music of the club, and Rachael did not feel compelled to pull away.

"I impressed you? That is high praise." Peter smirked down at Rachael and pulled her flush to his body. He wondered if she could feel the flutter of his heartbeat. "Listen, the situation with Kerry is complicated. It's not how she makes it out to be."

"Oh really? Then how is it?" Rachael quipped.

Peter wanted to phrase things in a way that wouldn't make him sound worse than the situation already did.

"I am never going to get back with her. I was always straight with her- no feelings, no permanent attachment. The whole thing was a mistake."

"Was it a mistake because she caught feelings, or was it a mistake because she already had a man?"

"Both. I should have considered just how messy it all would be. I'm not looking for another entanglement ever again."

"So are you saying that you are more than your reputation? Tell me about the real Peter Kane."

"I knew you were interested in me." Peter gave her a smoldering look and then laughed as Rachael rolled her eyes.

"I just want to believe that you are more than your reputation. We are partners, after all. I need to be able to trust you. Give me something to believe in."

The couple danced in silence for a moment. At any moment, either one of them could have stopped dancing or stopped touching, but it never crossed their minds to leave the bubble that they were creating on the dance floor.

"I have three sisters, Emma, Brielle, and Dara. A little brother, Darcy, who is Dara's twin. Then, of course, my mom, and two step-mothers. I love them to bits. My sister, Emma, is going to be a star, and I can't wait," Peter said, a look of pride radiating from his eyes as he spoke about his family. "Emma is a ballet dancer. She's loved dancing since she was a baby, and I'm so glad that I have been able to help support her. They're all amazing, really, but she's the oldest, and right now is her time to shine."

Rachael tilted her head, her waterfall of curls rolling off of her shoulder in luscious waves. She eyed him seriously. The intense look that she was giving him caused his heart to stop. At that moment, she was the most beautiful creature he had ever seen. She looked like a goddess. He was struck by her gorgeous chocolate brown eyes, the perfect cupid's bow of her lips. Even the way the constantly moving lights of the club danced against her dark amber skin.

"You're a family man at heart. I like that," Rachael said softly. "So, the time you spent speaking to my grandmother was the real you. You're just a big, tall, softy with a face that brings all the girls to the yard."

"What can I say? I love the ladies, and the older ladies just get me right here." He took their overlapped hands and tapped his heart. "You should find out what the buzz is all about."

"And.... You're back," Rachael said, shaking her head.

"C'mon... I've still gotta be me."

"I suppose you do."

They continued dancing. Rachael's arms were now draped around Peter's shoulders, his hands on her hips, his leg between her thighs.

"You mentioned your brother and sisters, your mom, and your step-moms. What about your dad?"

How could he explain the dynamic between him and Evan? It was tumultuous at the best of times and needy all of the time; whether it was him needing his father's love or his father needing his money.

"My dad is something else. Let's just say we don't always see life the same way."

"Dad's a bit problematic. Noted. I won't push the subject."

"It's fine. For you, I can be an open book. It's important to me that you really see me," Peter professed, voice earnest. "For the team dynamic, of course."

"Of course." Rachael grinned back. "How about we just dance for a while? No need to talk."

Peter just nodded in agreement and let the music sweep them away. Before they knew it, their dance had gone from intimate and questioning to downright sensual and knowing. Their bodies began to recognize each other in ways that words alone couldn't accomplish. There was a synchrony that they could only wish to achieve at the workplace. It was the dance of souls recognizing each other. They were so lost in the groove that it came as second nature for Rachel to rest her cheek against Peter's chest and for Peter's hands to slide down her back until one was caressing the curve of Rachael's butt, the other tangled in her hair. The beat slowed down, the lights dimmed, and without another thought, Rachael turned her face upward as he bent his down, inhaling her scent. Their lips called to each other. Just as they connected in the faintest of touches, a giggle was heard.

"Oh my!" Hendrick danced up to them, Kathy in his arms.

Peter and Rachael instantly took a step back. Their trance-like state was broken. Not only because their boss was observing them but also because they were shocked by the sight before them. Hendrick was dancing with Kathy, her leg wrapped around his waist. He was grinding against her like his life depended on it, and bringing up the rear was Señor Cartagena pressed against her, sandwiching Kathy between them, Pedro's hand guiding Kathy's hips rhythmically back and forth into Hendrick. Their jaws dropped as Hendrick spoke to them as if nothing odd was happening in front of his employees.

"Don't you just love this music? It's invigorating!" Mr. Pfeiffer said, pulling Kathy's leg even closer to his body. "So, tonight has been quite a success, don't you think?"

Peter could only bob his head up and down. He didn't know where to look.

"Anyway, why don't you contact Kathy in the morning, and you can make arrangements to meet with Señor Cartagena for later this week. We've had enough business for the night." With that said, Hendrick dropped Kathy's leg, spun her around toward Pedro Cartagena, and playfully slapped her ass as she wiggled it in his face.

"Uh, um. Yes, that sounds like a great idea. We should probably call it a night. After all, Peter and I don't want to be late tomorrow. It was so nice to meet you, Señor Cartagena. Peter and I will be in touch." Rachael was the first to recover and, much to Peter's relief, was able to speak coherently and get them out of the bizarro situation.

"Leaving so soon? Your dedication is noticed. It's for reasons like this that you are part of the cream of the crop at WCP. We will see you tomorrow, and don't forget to complete your report at the end of the week," Mr. Pfeiffer said. Having said that, Hendrick Pfeiffer, Kathy Starnes, and Pedro Cartagena danced away the most lascivious triad on the dance floor.

Chapter Twelve

ALL THE WAY HOME

Peter and Rachael left Hotel Brasilia's nightclub and made a quick escape to the Rivian. Once seated and buckled in the vehicle both let out a breath that they didn't realize they were holding and then burst into peals of laughter.

"Yo...." Rachael flopped back in the passenger seat tears forming at the corners of her eyes from laughter. "Umm... what was that?"

"Right? I'm not sure if that was strictly professional," Peter returned. "I couldn't get it together. You just don't see your CEO grinding away at his assistant like that every day."

"I'm not sure if that was strictly dancing," Rachael tittered. "I'm pretty sure we were somehow tangentially privy to some serious threesome foreplay."

"I was this close," Peter raised his fingers up in a pinching motion, "to shouting Eifel Tower! I was waiting for Pedro and Hendrick to high-five each other."

"I will never look at them the same again. How am I going to look Kathy in the face again? That woman is full of surprises."

"...and people worry about me being too sexual in the workplace. At least we were tasteful with everything." Peter laughed some more.

"I mean, sure, we almost kissed..." Rachael trailed off, fully realizing what had nearly transpired on the dance floor.

"Yeah, but that was tasteful," Peter continued to laugh and then glanced over at Rachael, and the laughter abruptly stopped. "I mean, obviously, it was just the music and the moment. We weren't really going to do it. It was those Latin rhythms. They just get you. Right?"

"Haha, yeah, you're right. It was just part of the dance. I mean, I don't go around kissing *anyone*, let alone my teammate at a nightclub." Rachael chuckled half-heartedly and then lapsed into silence.

Internally, Rachael was nothing but turmoil. She knew that it was more than just the music. They had nearly kissed. She had wanted to kiss Peter and the worst thing about it was that she still wanted to kiss him. She was relieved that Mr. Pfeiffer and his triad had interrupted them, but part of her was curious to know exactly what Peter's lips tasted like. Would he be a firm kisser, a coaxing kisser? Would he kiss and immediately repel her? God, she hoped that's what would happen. How could she be captivated by a man who was known for being the company lollipop- everyone had a lick? Plus, there was all of that Kerry baggage. That was just so much messiness. Rachael wasn't about that. Unfortunately, she was also seeing him in a different light. He loved his family, most of whom were women, so it stood to reason he didn't just see women as sex objects. Plus, he treated MiMi so sweetly and he hadn't even known that she was related to her. He was just being his authentic self at that moment. She wasn't interested in Peter "Sleazoid" Kane. Nope. No ma'am. That's what she was going to keep telling herself until it was true.

The ride to WCP was nearly at its end. After the initial bout of laughter, they both sat ruminating over the implications of their part in the evening's unexpected results. Peter broke the silence by bringing things back to a professional viewpoint.

"We still need to meet with Señor Cartagena one more time this week. Do you still want to do the botanical gardens?"

"Yes, I think that's a safe place. We keep it professional. Get down to the nitty gritty, find out what he's looking for from WCP. We'll collect the data and prepare a nice report for Mr. Pfeiffer and we will never speak of what we saw the three of them doing on that dance floor."

"I'll take it to the grave." Peter laughed.

They pulled up to the front entrance of the building, and Peter stopped the car.

"Do you need to go back inside for anything? I can walk with you." Peter said.

"No, I'm good. I don't need to go back up. Thank you."

"Where's your scooter? Or did you bring a car today?"

"I'm fine. Don't worry about me. I'll get home okay," Rachael claimed. "I plan on taking a rideshare back to my place."

Peter frowned. "You don't need to do that. I'm more than happy to drive you home. Please. I'll feel better knowing you made it to your door safely. Remember, we're teammates, and we don't let our teammates fail."

Rachael sighed. "Fine. I'm not far."

She punched her address into Peter's GPS, and they rode the extra fifteen minutes together, making inane small chat. Rachael was inexplicably nervous about letting him drive her home. There was no reason for it, but it felt like she was bringing him closer to her private world, and she wasn't sure if she was ready for that or if she even wanted it.

"Well, here we are," Peter said as he pulled up to her adorable yellow cottage. Her home was located on a side street that held a combination of Cape Cods and Colonial-style houses that were clearly built mid-century. They still had the quality building materials like stone and brick rather than simply the aesthetically appealing but structurally pointless facing.

"Thank you, Peter," Rachael said as she opened the passenger door. She hesitated, feeling she ought to invite him in for a nightcap, but this wasn't a date. This was work, and she had to keep that in mind. "I'll see you tomorrow. We're friends, you know. I promise I won't ride you so hard anymore."

"Oh, I don't know... that ride doesn't sound so bad," Peter tempted. He gave her a wink and then laughed.

"Man! You're always playing. I can't with you," Rachael giggled. "Have a good night." She shut the door and went up her walkway. She unlocked the door and turned back to see Peter watching her. She waved to let him know she was safe and then went inside to tell Risky Business all about her night.

Chapter Thirteen

HOW DOES YOUR GARDEN GROW?

Rachael stood as Señor Cartagena entered the Dashwood Gardens Tea Room.

"Buenos Dias, Señor Cartagena"

"Buenos Dias, Raquel, chica bella," Pedro replied, grasping Rachael's hands in a friendly gesture.

"It's so good to see you again, Pedro. I'm looking forward to showing you our gardens. Peter and I had a great time with you."

"Ah yes, Peter. Have you given my words any thought? I saw the way you were together. You two will be perfect together."

"Oh, Pedro," Rachael laughed. "That was just the music. We got caught up in the moment. I assure you there's nothing there. You'll see when he arrives."

"Perhaps, perhaps. You know where there's smoke..." Pedro began.

"There's fire." Rachael completed.

"Indeed, but for you? It's an inferno. Trust me."

Pedro placed his arm around Rachael's waist and pulled her in for a fatherly hug and kiss on the cheek.

"Excuse me, *Señor.*" Peter firmly clamped a hand on Pedro's shoulder. Pedro winced at the impact. "I'm sure you don't need to constantly touch Rachael to conduct our business."

"Hello, Peter," Pedro stepped out of Peter's grasp and extended his hand. "It is good to see you again."

Peter shook his hand, holding it longer than necessary. "A pleasure. Let's make sure it's a pleasure for everyone and only touch when invited."

"Peter!" Rachael gasped out. "I'm fine. Pedro and I were having a lovely conversation."

"Hmph," was Peter's only response.

"Okay. Anyway, Pedro," Rachael shot Peter an irritated look. "Would you like to tour the grounds first or have lunch now?"

Pedro gave Rachael a sly smile.

"Let us eat first, Raquel. The flowers will be there, but I would love to get my fill of looking at your beauty first."

Rachael blushed, looking down at her hands before smiling back at Señor Cartagena. "Thank you, Pedro. Our table is right over here."

Rachael led them over to a lovely, well-lit corner of the tea room surrounded by magnolias, bougainvillea, and hyacinths. The table was set with tea sandwiches, cakes, and pots of tea in various flavors.

"This is lovely, so lovely, Raquel." Pedro beamed and patted her hand. Peter simply scowled at Pedro and angrily placed his napkin on his lap. Rachael was completely perplexed by his behavior. From her perspective, Pedro was the sweetest man. They continued their lunch, and Pedro did everything he could to make sure Rachael was comfortable, opening jars of jam for her and pouring her cups of tea. He couldn't do enough for her, and the more he did, the more Peter's expression darkened. Very little business was discussed. Instead, they were regaled with tales of Honduras and Pedro's life growing up.

"You wouldn't believe how beautiful our beaches are, cara mia. You must come to visit me, Raquel," Pedro said. "And you as well, Peter." The addition of Peter was clearly an afterthought given purely out of politeness only.

"Okay, first, her name is Rachael, not *Raquel* or Carrie Mia or whatever you're calling her. Can we finally talk business, or do you need to flirt a little bit more?" Peter said, tossing his napkin on the table.

"Peter," Rachael said sternly. "Pedro is our client."

"Oh, it's Pedro now? What is going on here?" He pushed himself away from the table and ran his hand over his face in a frustrated motion. "Listen, I need to step away for a moment. Sorry, Señor Cartagena. I'll be back. I have to make a phone call."

Rachael watched in shocked consternation as Peter walked away.

"Pedro, I'm so sorry," Rachael began.

"Sorry?" Pedro laughed. "No need. I am delighted! You see? You see? He is burning for you!"

Rachael looked at Pedro and blinked, then burst into laughter.

"Pedro! You're killing me. You've been laying it on extra thick just to get at Peter!"

Pedro just grinned at her.

"What can I say, Raquelita? I love love, and I see good things for you two. Peter just needs to see what he's missing." He shrugged, palms raised.

"Um, I think I need to be on board for this love to happen," Rachael challenged.

"Love finds a way," Pedro insisted.

Just then, Peter returned to the table with a more placid expression on his face.

"Señor Cartagena, I apologize. Let's take a walk around the gardens and resume our business."

"Of course. Please, call me Pedro."

"Pedro, Rachael," Peter stood and pulled out her chair. "Let me show you some of our exotic blooms." Peter was careful to place himself between Rachael and Pedro and kept his hand at the small of her back possessively.

They finished their afternoon in the gardens, acquiring the details that they would need for their report. The whole afternoon left Rachael feeling uneasy. Peter had made sure to stay in some form of physical contact with her for the rest of the day. It was as though he couldn't stand to not have some form of connection with her for even a second. She wanted to be furious with him for potentially putting their assignment in jeopardy, but she couldn't deny that Peter was now occupying a disproportionate amount of space in her mind. Even once she was back home, his touches lingered all over her body.

Rachael sat on her sofa reading with Risky on her lap when her phone buzzed, informing her that she had a text.

Peter: Hi Rachael

Rachael: Hey

Rachael couldn't imagine what this man wanted. Their business was done, and she really needed some space from him. She could see that he was typing for a long time but nothing was sent. She put her phone down and went back to reading. Her phone buzzed again.

Peter: Just wanted to apologize about earlier today. Pedro was out of line.

Rachael sat up. This man was crazy.

Rachael: Excuse me? The only one out of line today was you. You were rude to our client. You're just fortunate that Pedro is a sweet man and won't report you to Mr. Pfeiffer.

Peter: Sweet? He's handsy. I'm not letting anyone take advantage of you.

Rachael: Again. I can take care of myself. I'm grown. You don't need to do it for me.

Peter: You weren't, so I did it for you.

Rachael: You need to sort yourself out. Get therapy and leave me alone!

Rachael turned off her notifications and tossed her phone on the coffee table. She was done with the conversation, and she was done with Peter Kane.

Chapter Fourteen

RING A DING DING, THE TELEPHONE RINGS

"How's my favorite grandbaby?" MiMi sounded excited over the phone.

"Hi, MiMi. I'm good. What's got you so chipper this morning?" Rachael asked.

"I'm just excited to see you tomorrow night. I ordered your Pops's favorite pineapple upside-down cheesecake. I can't wait to hear all about your week!" MiMi gushed.

"Yummy! I'm extra excited now, too. That cake is delicious! You got it from Ms. Betty at the Ladies' Club?"

"You know I did. It's not worth eating if it's not made by her. Now, tell me about your week!! I know you had to see that good-looking young man."

"Yeah, I saw him. Listen, I know you think he's pretty and all, but his good looks aren't enough to overcome that personality. He's just the worst!" Rachael said emphatically.

"Really? He was a true gentleman when I met him. What did he do wrong?" MiMi asked.

Rachael relayed everything, well, almost everything that happened at both Hotel Brasilia and Dogwood Gardens.

"You see? He's the worst. He seems to think he can treat me like a poor dumb woman, and then he wants to control and patronize me."

"Is that what you think's happening? How do you figure? From what you tell me, he's just trying to be a man and protect you."

"From what? My job. No, MiMi, he's a controlling dick!"

"Language!"

"Sorry, MiMi. I only swear like this when he comes up as a topic of conversation. First, I said asshole around you, and now I'm saying dick. It's Peter's fault."

"You're still saying them, Rachael." MiMi said with a firm edge in her voice. "I know you weren't raised to speak to your elders like that."

"You're right. I'm sorry."

"Sounds to me like he likes you, and he's showing you the best way he knows how, by making sure you're not being taken advantage of. If you ask me, you need to stop thinking of him as a controlling dick and learn to control that dick!"

"MiMi!!!"

"What did I tell you last time, baby? I'm MiMi. I can say it. *You* can't." MiMi fell out laughing. "Alright baby, see you tomorrow after work."

MiMi Palmer ended the conversation thoroughly amused.

* * *

Rachael's Granny: Hi, Mr. Kane. Do you remember me? I met you at the pharmacy two weeks ago. I'm Rachael's grandmother, Bess Palmer.

Drugstore Hottie: Hi, Mrs. Palmer. I remember you very well. It's good to hear from you. How's your hip doing?

Rachael's Granny: Oh, my hip's fine, honey, but that's not why I'm texting you. We would love to have you over for dinner tomorrow night.

Drugstore Hottie: Really? I would love to come over. Are you sure Rachael doesn't mind?

Rachael's Granny: We would love to have you! I'll send my address! We can't wait to see you. Goodnight!

Peter sat back in his chair and grinned. He wasn't sure if Rachael knew it or not, but he was about to become a big part of her life. He couldn't wait for dinner.

Chapter Fifteen

ELEVATE

It had been a long day and Rachael couldn't wait to get out of the office and over to her grandparents' house. They were just what she needed after the week she'd had. Between her regular tasks, entertaining Señor Cartagena, and trying to create some version of a professional report in regards to what WCP could expect from Pedro her mind was fried. The biggest obstacle to her peace of mind and relaxation was Peter, though. Every time she thought she'd made headway and gotten to a place where she could not only tolerate him but possibly like him, he messed it up. She was still fuming about their text conversation from several nights ago when she got on the elevator to leave WCP.

"Little Bird, we have to stop meeting like this."

Of course it was him. There was no other person who would call her that or that she wanted to avoid more than Peter. If she were honest, it wasn't because he got on her nerves, either.

"I'm not talking to you," she scolded and stood as far away from him as she could.

"That's okay. I can talk for both of us." He grinned at her and then proceeded to carry on a one-sided conversation. "I had a great day, thank you for asking. Hmm? You're right. I'm just as handsome as I am nice. You shouldn't say such naughty things! What will people think?"

"You can stop that right now," Rachael interrupted.

"Stop what? It's not my fault that you just can't stop thinking of me. You want to touch me where? Rachael, this is a place of business!" he said in mock outrage.

Rachael walked up to him and flicked him in the ear.

"How's that for a touch! How do you like that? Now be quiet for the rest of the ride."

"Ouch! I didn't like that at all. Come and kiss it and make it better," Peter flirted.

This man! Rachael thought. *I ought to kiss him just to shut him up and shock him.*

The elevator doors opened, and someone got on the elevator. Peter pretended to zipper his mouth shut while Rachael just gave him an evil grin back. She was certain she had the perfect way to get back at him. They went down another floor, and their intruder exited.

"Now, about this injury you just inflicted-" Peter began in a teasing tone. His words were cut off, and the breath caught in his throat. As soon as the doors closed, Rachael leaped at him, causing him to fall against the wall of the elevator. She reached for his head, curled her fingers in his hair, and pulled him down for a quick, hard kiss.

"Ha! Now, who's laughing?" Rachael said.

She looked over at Peter in triumph, and immediately stopped laughing. His eyes had gone from merriment to a sapphire smolder. He pressed the stop button on the elevator panel and walked over to her like a panther after its prey. Smooth and full of intent. She was captivated by the look in his eyes.

"Little Bird, if you wanted to kiss me, all you had to do was say the word."

Peter ran a finger down her cheek and neck and then traced the delicate curve of her collarbone. Leaning in, he placed a soft, warm kiss on her plump lips. Nipping and tasting her mouth teasingly, then possessively moving his lips across hers. Her hands instinctively pulled at his shirt, tugging it from the confines of his waistband. This kiss was everything she feared— hot, confident, possessive, masterful. It was everything she didn't know she had been craving. Her hands slipped under his shirt, gliding over the firm planes of his abs, sliding upward to feel his pecs. She couldn't get enough of his skin and his kisses. The more she touched his body, the deeper and more fervent his kisses became, moving from her lips to her cheek and licking down her neck. She whimpered at the sensation. Peter reacted to that sweet sound by picking her up, wrapping her legs around his waist, and pushing her against the wall to kiss and grind all of his intentions and desires into her valley.

Rachael could no longer think, at that moment, her world began and ended everywhere that their bodies connected. She thrust her hips forward to meet his rotating hips. Peter let out a moan that bordered on a growl.

"Rachael," he rasped.

"Shut up. Just keep kissing me."

"As you wish." He proceeded to kiss her more, unfastening the top buttons of her blouse so that he could place kisses and bites at the top of her breasts.

"You taste so good," he said.

Things may have continued to progress had there not come an insistent buzzing and a crackling voice through the elevator speaker.

"Is everything okay? We're sending maintenance to assist. Please respond," a tiny voice said.

Peter and Rachael froze, trying to catch their breaths.

"Oh no!" Rachael mouthed.

"Everything's fine," Peter announced, sounding unflustered. "My bag accidentally hit the stop button. No maintenance required. My apologies."

"Are you certain? They've already been dispatched. I can recall them if you are certain," the voice said.

"Yes, I am certain," Peter said as he placed Rachael back on her feet and started adjusting her clothing.

"Okay. Please depress the button, and the elevator will start moving again."

"10-4," Peter replied.

Peter tucked his shirt and pressed the button. Rachael refused to look him in the eye. She had never planned on things going that way. The elevator resumed its crawl to the next floor. The doors opened to a patiently waiting Mr. Pfeiffer.

"Ah, two of my favorites! I see you've learned how to play nice together," Hendrick chuckled.

Rachael looked at Mr. Pfeiffer, not quite understanding what he was hinting at.

"I see your confusion. Perhaps I can help you." He pulled out his pocket square and wiped at the corner of Peter's mouth. "I believe this belongs to you?"

He showed the cloth to Rachael, who visibly blanched with embarrassment. Her lipstick was all over the piece of fabric.

"I, I-" Rachael stammered. "I'm late for dinner with my grandmother. Have a wonderful night, Mr. Pfeiffer," Rachael blurted and then sprinted off the elevator.

"This isn't the floor to the garage!" Mr. Pfeiffer called after her and then practically collapsed in giggles.

Chapter Sixteen

EVAN CALLS

Peter rushed to catch Rachael as she exited the elevator. A large, strong hand gripped his arm.

"Peter," Hendrick commanded. "Let her go. If I've learned nothing in life, it's that you have to let a woman feel comfortable in her choices and know that she has command of where her life is going."

It was a rare moment of seriousness from Mr. Hendrick Pfeiffer and it gave Peter pause. He turned back and looked at Hendrick.

"Don't look so skeptical. I don't just observe my employees, I observe life! If you want the prize, you have to know the race you're in and train for it. Now, go get your team-building skills together."

Peter wanted to tell his boss that he was really weird but thought better of it. It was too late to chase after Rachael, and he would see her at her grandparent's house.

"Thanks for that advice, Hendrick. I have a surprise dinner date to get to."

* * *

Peter pulled into his garage and entered his house through the pantry. He walked through his immaculate house, thanks to his housecleaner Theodora. He glanced around at the immaculately designed home and, for the first time, realized he could actually have more in his life. Peter could see her in his house, her multicolored waves adding a slash of brightness to his hyper-masculine grey, black, and brown interior. Her curves would add the softness that his angular industrial décor lacked. With the taste of Rachael's skin on his tongue and the sizzle of the crush of their mouths dancing across his lips, he felt the after-shocks of their encounter. He never experienced anything like that before. In all his experience with women, he always had the upper hand. He enjoyed them, but he never caught feelings or felt that explicit zing that he had heard so much about. He was out of his depths and wanted someone to talk to but being a lady's man had alienated him from any close male friends. Women were out of the question because they were either mad to be with him or mad that they weren't with him. Except for Rachael, she generally was just mad at him... and he just thought it was the cutest thing. Still, it would have been nice to have someone to talk to.

Peter's phone buzzed as he stood in front of the bathroom mirror, debating whether or not to shave completely or just trim his beard to keep the lines sharp. He glanced down at the screen and groaned. When he said he wanted someone to talk to, his father, Evan, was not who he had in mind.

"Buddy boy!" his father said in greeting.

"Hi, Dad. What's up?"

"Just calling to check on my oldest son."

Peter was glad that he wasn't on a video call. The face he made would have insulted his father.

"Listen, son. I need your help. Emma started dance classes, but now Brielle has club basketball. You think you can spot me? I'm good for it."

"Spot you? Did you already promise her?"

"Of course, I promised her. You've got to keep the ladies happy. I can't give to Emma and not give to the others."

Peter groaned. How many times would Evan promise what he can't deliver to his sisters.?

"You got a job then, right? If you are good for it then I know you're working," Peter said.

"Why do you keep bringing that up whenever I ask you for the smallest thing? Yes, I got a gig coming up. I'm waiting for the callback."

"Okay. That's great, Dad. I'm glad you might have an acting gig, but I'm talking about a real job. Work. 9 to 5."

"You know I can't do that. Then they're all going to want child support. I'm not an ATM. They'll all constantly be begging me for money. Can you even imagine what that would be like? Hell, I'm not about that life."

"No, I can't possibly imagine what that would be like," Peter deadpanned.

"Anyway, Sadie's been up my ass, complaining that I'm all over the place, not stopping by enough, not giving her kids enough attention. There's nothing like a nagging woman. I tell you, kid, you take after me in two ways, and you're smarter than me in one."

"Oh boy, I can't wait to hear this," Peter huffed.

"You've got my looks and a killer way with the ladies. You're just like me. You can get any woman you want. You're smarter than me, though, because you learned and applied what I've always told you. You get in, and you get out. Enjoy a woman, but never get too attached. It's not worth it. Look at me. I have all this baggage- kids, debt. They always want something. Being with me should be enough, but all women want is to trap you. I've gotta be free, no what I mean? That's why I'm proud of you. You're free as a bird, no long-term attachments, and what you have is yours. You don't have to answer or give it to anybody."

"I have to give it all to you, Dad," Peter quipped. "Last week, it was $4000. How much this week? After a while, I won't have anything left."

"I only need $1500. That's pennies for a big shot like you."

Peter seethed inside.

"Dad, that's $5500 in two weeks. What is going on? I can't do it. I'm sorry."

"Come on. I already promised. It'll break Brielle's heart. You want me to tell your sister I can't do it and that you were willing to help your favorite sister, Emma, but not her? I guess it's okay for the others to know that they can't count on you. Please, help your pop out."

"Dad.... I don't have a favorite sister. Why would you even say something like that? You can really be a bastard sometimes. Let me see what I can do."

"That's my boy. I always said you were my favorite! You take after me, and you know what you owe."

Evan sounded so cheerful as he ended the call. In contrast, Peter felt muddled with a sense of guilt, duty, and dread. Was he really that much like Evan Kane?

Chapter Seventeen

DO YOU WANT IT ON YOUR COLLARD GREENS

Rachael lifted the lid off the pot of mixed turnip, kale, and collard greens that simmered on the stove. She inhaled deeply, enjoying the aroma of the smoked turkey butt and leafy greens. Nothing smelled like comfort and home as much as MiMi Palmer's greens. She could use a little comfort. Her nerves were in a state of flux after her ride in the elevator.

"Oooh!!! MiMi! They smell so good. What's so special that we're getting your greens on a work night?" Rachael asked as she replaced the lid.

MiMi Palmer shuffled over to the stove and lightly popped Rachael on the hand.

"Put that lid down and let it simmer! Keep all that goodness in that pot. You know your Pops likes a glass of warm pot liquor before he goes to bed."

MiMi bent over to check the oven window. "Mmhmm. That macaroni and cheese is getting to be a real nice golden brown. Now, why do you think there has to be a special occasion? Can't I just make my grandbaby a nice meal? Now help me set this table."

Rachael grabbed three plates from the cabinet and started to set the table.

"No, not those. Get the nice ones with the gold trim," MiMi said.

Rachael turned and put the plain plates back in the cabinet and gave her grandmother the side-eye.

"What's wrong with our usual plates? This is weird. You didn't even wait for me to get over here and help you cook, MiMi."

"I'm just feeling fancy tonight. Ain't nothing wrong with the regular plates. I just want to be fancy. Matter of fact, why don't you go on upstairs and rest? I know you had a busy day today. Oh! I ordered something for you, why don't you try it on. It's upstairs in the bedroom."

Rachael frowned and continued to stare at MiMi. "This is just... why are you acting like this? This is not how we do Wednesday night dinners."

"Girl! What did I say? Now go on up there and get yourself freshened up and then come down and show me that cute outfit I got you. Go on!"

Rachael grumbled as she followed her grandmother's orders and headed up to see what MiMi Palmer had purchased for her. She would have protested more, but she welcomed the few moments of distracted solitude that she was about to get. Despite wanting to be focused on dinner with MiMi and Pops, Rachael could not stop thinking about how everything had gotten flipped in the elevator. Truth be told, had security not interrupted, she wasn't so sure if she wouldn't have been the one flipped around in the most delicious way. And that's what upset her. She wasn't supposed to like Peter's kisses, and she damn sure wasn't supposed to spend the rest of the afternoon fantasizing about the way he ground against her in that elevator. It was possessive, hot, and intense. If he could work her up that much with just an elevator kiss, she hated to think what he could do when there was time and space. Most importantly, this was PETER!!! He was so icky. He was a womanizer. She couldn't stand him. He didn't know the meaning of a relationship. Rachael's thoughts continued to spiral. Unbidden, dancing with him popped into mind. She closed her eyes and imagined being held close by him and then recreating that moment when they had nearly kissed.

Now she could fill in the blanks, and she had to admit the real thing was way better than she could ever have imagined.

"Girl!" Rachael said out loud, chastising herself. "Get it together."

She opened the bedroom door and saw two bags and a tissue-wrapped package tied with a ribbon sitting on the bed. She opened one and saw a royal blue satin bra and matching panties. The blue matched the peacock shade of blue in her hair perfectly. Next, she unwrapped the tissue paper package and discovered a dress that MiMi had made for her. It was a royal peacock blue. The dress had a slightly plunging, draped neckline. It was a really pretty color. If nothing else, MiMi Palmer could sew! She had an amazing fashion sense. Rachael laid out all of the garments on the bed and admired them. She opened the last bag and discovered that it held a pair of strappy satin heels in a lighter shade of blue, almost a turquoise green. It was a gorgeous outfit.

I wonder what made MiMi put this outfit together for me, Rachael thought to herself.

"Baby, did you find everything? You see that dress I made for you?" MiMi Palmer called up the stairs.

"Yes, MiMi. I love the colors! Thank you, MiMi !" Rachael called back.

"Well, hurry up and put it on. I want to see how it all looks on you. Put everything on, too. You know a dress is only as good as the foundation underneath it!"

Rachael undressed and quickly put on the outfit, noting that the bra was a push-up and the panties had substantial tummy support. Next, she pulled the dress over her head. The smooth, cool, light-weight satin fabric slid like liquid over her body, clinging to her breasts, hips, and bust- yet somehow only skimming over her tummy. She put on her heels and walked to the full-length mirror that hung on the back of the bedroom door. Rachael's jaw dropped. MiMi Palmer had outdone herself. She looked amazing. The dress was sexy and flirty without being too clubbish. It was a perfect dress to impress on a date night or a night of dancing. The draped neckline allowed her cleavage to show while the bra kept the girls sitting high and full. Every curve popped. The heels were the right height, elongating her lean legs yet allowing the curve of her calf muscles to appear enhanced without being completely activated in a tightly flexed muscle. She looked so good, she thought she might try something a little fun with her hair and took the ribbon from the package, pulled her waved tresses to the side, and tied them in a low pony so that they hung over her shoulder, the shaved side of her head left bare.

"Rachael! Come on, now! I want to see you!" MiMi called again.

"Here I come!" Rachael folded up her discarded work clothes and placed them in one of the bags, then left the bedroom.

Too bad I didn't have this outfit on when we went to Hotel Brasilia, Rachael thought. *Too bad I don't have anywhere or anyone to show this off to."*

"MiMi! You really did your thing with this dress-"

Rachael was interrupted by the sound of her grandmother's giggles mingled with male laughter that was distinctly not her Pops's raspy chuckle. She knew that rich laugh. *Oh God, please, no.* Rachael started to backpedal up the stairs, but it was too late, MiMi Palmer had seen her.

"There she is. There's my baby girl! Isn't she gorgeous?"

"She sure is," Peter looked her over from top to toe, managing to somehow to look like he wanted to devour her but also looking completely respectful all at once. How he managed that feat was a mystery to Rachael. "It's good to see you again, Rachael."

"Good to see you too, Peter," Rachael mumbled. "MiMi, can I see you in the kitchen?"

"Now?" MiMi asked.

"Yes, right now," Rachael demanded through gritted teeth and turned to head toward the kitchen, grateful that the kitchen was in the back of the house.

The two Palmer women walked to the kitchen, one stalking angrily and swaying her hips in a way that was sure to keep Peter's eyes focused on the main attraction. The other walked slowly, with a satisfied grin on her face.

"What is he doing here?" Rachael asked, pacing back and forth in front of the stove.

"Sit down, girl, before you fall and hurt yourself," MiMi pulled out a chair at the table and gestured for Rachael to sit. "Now, what's the problem?"

"My problem is that the asshole is here. In your living room. On *our* dinner night. Why is he here?" Rachael asked, voice rising an octave higher on the last word.

"I would think it was obvious. I like him. I like him for you and he sure is pretty to look at." MiMi grinned.

"But you promised you wouldn't invite him over!" Rachael whined, her inner teenager leaking out. "Why didn't you keep your promise?"

"I most certainly did keep my promise. If you recall, my exact words were I wouldn't invite him over *that week*. I didn't invite him over that week. I invited him this week."

"You knew what I meant. I can't believe we're arguing over semantics. You know I can't stand that man. I see him all the time- at work, after work, team building exercises. I deserve a break from him!"

"You really can't stand him?" MiMi gave her a shrewd look.

"I really can't."

"Well, are you seeing any other man? Going on any dates?"

"You know I'm not. I would have told you, MiMi."

"So, what you're telling me is that Peter is just this asshole that you spend all of your time with at work, sometimes after work, and you aren't seeing *anybody* else?"

Rachael shook her head.

"Okay. You don't like him, and he's the only man around you. So how do you explain this?" MiMi asked and lightly brushed a spot at the curve of Rachael's shoulder and neck.

"Explain what?" Rachael asked.

"The love bite on your neck," MiMi said plainly, eyebrow raised in question.

"Wha- what are you talking about?" Rachael stuttered.

"See for yourself."

Rachael walked over to the sink, looked at the mirrored cabinetry, and gasped. There, on her shoulder, was a darkened patch of skin that could be mistaken for nothing except a hickey. Her mind flashed back to their encounter on the elevator. She let out a little gasp as she recalled the kisses that trailed down her neck, Peter's tongue licking and nipping above her shoulder. Catching herself sliding too deeply into that memory, she frowned. See, this is why he's an asshole. He just *had* to leave a mark. That man wouldn't know discreet if it slapped him in the face.

"Now tell me, if you aren't seeing any man recreationally and you're only ever around Peter, right? Then who gave you that hickey, huh?"

Rachael glanced down at the floor.

"Look at you. You can't even look me in the eye. Tell me again how much you don't like him?"

"Mimi, he's awful-"

"I think you need to tell that to someone who doesn't already know. You may not want to like him, and he might just be an asshole, but I think you need to give him a chance. At the very least, let's have some fun with him for dinner. If he turns out to be as horrible as you say, I'll never mention his name again. If not, well... let's just say I'm looking forward to having some cute little mixed great-grandbabies. What is he mixed with, by the way? He's an exotic look about himself. Right now, I'm calling him Spicy White."

Rachael just shook her head, palm covering her face. What could she say? Her grandmother had her dead to rights. She had kissed him, and even she had to admit every now and then, she saw a glimmer in Peter that wasn't the worst.

"Fine. We'll have this dinner, but I'm pretty sure he's going to show his ass, and Pops won't be able to stand him. Then you'll finally understand," Rachael retorted.

"Uh-huh. We'll see," was all MiMi said.

"And let's not go crazy, talking about great-grandbabies. Spicy white!" Rachael laughed and shook her head. "Alright, you've won this round. Let's get back to the living room. I'm curious to see if Pops is ready to kick him out already."

* * *

Peter stood in the living room watching Rachael and Bess Palmer walk away toward the kitchen, contemplating just how extraordinarily beautiful his teammate was. There was just something about her that he couldn't get enough of, which is why he had lost some of his control in the elevator. That little taste she gave him wasn't enough. She was cute, thinking that little kiss was teaching him a lesson. Little did she know, he had a lesson plan for her that he had been subconsciously dying to show her. And he did. He had pushed that kiss to the limit and her response had been better than he could have hoped. Peter couldn't thank Bess Palmer enough for this opportunity to push his advantage.

"That's right. My Bess is a beautiful woman."

Peter turned his head at the sound of Pops Palmer's voice.

"Your wife certainly is, and she's quite a character," Peter added.

Pops sat back in his armchair and leveled a cool stare at Peter, seeming to asses him from head to toe and returning to look him in the eye.

"So, you're the man Bess has picked out for Rachael, huh? While they're in the kitchen, let me learn you a little something."

Peter didn't dare speak, sensing that he needed to hear what Mr. Palmer was going to say.

"Women, goddesses, like Bess and Rachael aren't to be played with. I've overheard enough of their conversations to know that you spend most of your time using them like toys. But that's not how a man behaves. Running through the women, never developing anything real, is a one-way ticket to unhappiness and when you get to be my age- sheer loneliness." Pops leaned forward in his chair to get closer as he lowered his voice. "That's what I would say about a basic woman. I see the way you watched Rachael just now, and let me tell you, she is special. There's nothing simple or basic about her. She needs to be loved, cherished, listened to, and understood. She doesn't play games, and she doesn't chase after a man, so if you want to be with her, understand she won't entertain your foolishness, but she'll be solid to the end if you treat her right. Show her that you're more than the 'Drug Store Hottie'."

"Sir, I-" Peter started.

Pops cut him off. "Call me Pops. Listen, I was like you when I was a young man. I had girls falling all over me, and I ate it up. Bounced from one to the other, careless of the repercussions then I saw Bess, and it was a wrap. I had to chase *her*, and she put me through my paces, boy!" Pops chuckled at the memory. "Point is I had to grow up and wise up to keep her, and if you want to be with and keep Rachael? I already know. You've got to do better than what you're doing now. Understand?"

Peter was caught off guard by Pops' words but they had a whole lot of truth to them. He thought about his father and how he lived his life, in contrast to this older man before him who was clearly content with the same woman that he had been with for decades. He wanted a life like that, not running into his fifties like Evan, flirting with anything with a hint of beauty. He hadn't fully articulated his feelings for Rachael to himself but he couldn't refute that he wanted more from Rachael. It just took Pops to solidify what was right there on the surface for him. It wasn't worth resisting, and he felt his whole physical bearing shift in acquiescence. Gone was the cocky swagger for a moment as he locked eyes with Pops and nodded.

"I understand. Foolish games are all in the past."

"Alright now! That's what I like to hear. Do you know anything about spades?" Pops asked.

As it happened, Peter was an excellent spades player. He and Pops Palmer were playing and enjoying themselves like old friends when Rachael and MiMi Palmer returned to the living room.

"John, you got that boy playing spades?" MiMi asked in shock.

"Why not? He's good at it and you two were fussing about in the kitchen. My boy, Peter here, knows how to play!" Pops laughed.

"I told you he was spicy!" MiMi said and nudged Rachael.

Peter looked up to see Rachael gawking at the scene, mouth slightly open in shock. He shot her a grin and winked at her before folding his cards over onto the coffee table and standing up to greet her.

"Hi, Rachael. You look amazing."

He noticed color rise to her cheeks and she absent-mindedly stroked her neck, drawing his eye to the mark he left on her in the elevator. He felt heat rush to his face as well.

"Peter. I never expected to actually see you here."

They stared at each other for a moment. Peter started to reach to touch the spot on her neck but was interrupted by MiMi Palmer.

"Dinner is served. Let's go to the dining room and have a nice meal! And Peter- Rachael helped. You're going to love our home cooking." MiMi said as she shuffled to the kitchen as everyone followed, Rachael bringing up the rear, grumbling to herself.

Once everyone was seated, Pops and MiMi were at the head of the table, Rachael and Peter across from each other. The conversation flowed freely from Rachael's grandparents, but fewer than four words passed between Rachael and Peter. He tried to make eye contact with her but she studiously avoided his eye and focused on her meal. Occasionally, she would turn to speak to either Pops or Mimi, and he had time to study her in earnest, The curve of her lips as she laughed at something they said. He was even enamored with the way her throat bobbed as she swallowed her meal. He particularly liked how the low, side ponytail she wore rested on the opposite shoulder of the love mark that he had left on her neck. Normally, he would never have done such a thing, but the idea of that mark clearly claiming her as his pleased him. He smiled to himself, forgetting for a moment that he was not alone. He was roused from reverie by chuckles from opposite ends of the table.

"Peter. Peter!"

"Hmm. I'm sorry. I missed that," Peter admitted, pulling him from his distraction.

"Do you want it on your collard greens?" Rachael asked.

"Excuse me?"

"This hot sauce. Do you want some on your greens? That's how we like them."

"Rachael, baby, he can't help himself. He's too busy staring at that love bite he put on your neck!" MiMi burst into laughter.

"Mimi!!!!" Rachael exclaimed.

"Come on now, Bess, don't embarrass them like that. They have to figure this thing out on their own. Don't go agitating them," Pops laughed. "You don't want me to start telling stories about our courtship, do you?"

"I do not!" MiMi snapped. "But it's not my fault that he's acting like a teenager with his first crush."

Peter felt like he should be embarrassed by this extremely awkward moment, but he was too busy taking a bit of pleasure from Rachael's reaction. She was glaring at her grandmother and looked like she was about to protest. *The lady protests too much,* Peter thought.

"Don't you say a word, Rachael. You're no better than he is. I see the way you're glancing at him when you don't think anyone's looking.

I don't know why you're so embarrassed. That's a good-looking man right there!"

Peter had to chuckle. Rachael's MiMi was hilarious and had zero filter. He knew she was a spitfire when they had met at the drugstore. Rachael looked like she was about to burst, so he decided it would be a good time to change the subject.

"Did Rachael tell you that we're partners at work?"

"She sure did. Going to botanical gardens, dancing at Hotel Brasilia. Sounds a lot like some really cute dates to me. You can call it work if you want to, but I know a date," MiMi replied.

"Uh, Peter," Pops interrupted. "Tell me a little bit about yourself. Do you have any brothers or sisters?"

Peter paused mid-bite. He hadn't planned on speaking about his family. He had just started to forget about the phone call with his father and relax into this chaotic dinner. Now, the looming specter of his father and his womanizing ways was about to be on full display. He felt the charming mask slip from his face for a moment, then in a blink, he pulled back that winning flirtatious smile and answered.

"I do. I have three sisters. All younger than me. They're great. I also have one little brother."

"That's a nice big family. Mmm! All those girls must have made getting ready for school rough," Pops gathered.

"Ah, not too bad. I didn't actually spend any time with them all at once growing up. I lived with my mother, and they each stayed with their moms. My youngest siblings are actually twins. My mom had them when I was in college." Peter cleared his throat and looked down at his plate. "This mac and cheese is amazing, MiMi Bess."

"I see. Well, I'm sure you have your hands full with all of them," Pops replied.

"I do. They're all into different things. I try to support them whenever I can. The oldest, Emma, is a ballerina. She's so good. Perhaps I can treat you all to one of her performances." Pride radiated from his expression. "Brielle, my second stepmom's daughter, is into the arts as well. She's an actress and a basketball player. You would think her grace on the court would transfer to dance, but she has no rhythm. The moment dance music starts, it's like she has two left feet," Peter chuckled.

Rachael looked at him with rapt attention. He had mentioned his family before but this was the first time she was getting a deeper glimpse into what made Peter tick.

"So, let me get this straight. Your daddy had three wives. Did I hear that correctly?" MiMi asked.

"Yes, ma'am," Peter answered. "My mother, Caroline, Sadie, and my mom again."

"And your mama came back for seconds? Your Daddy must be rich or really good-looking. Ideally, both," MiMi marveled.

"He's... he's something else," Peter frowned. "Definitely not rich. He gave up a burgeoning successful acting and modeling career when I came along. He loves reminding me."

"Have I seen him in anything? That's kind of exciting!" MiMi said. "John, our Rachael is going to be part of a celebrity family!"

"Woah!!! Hang on now, Mimi! Peter and I are coworkers. That's it!" Rachael interjected.

"Hush. I'm having fun, baby," MiMi said and then turned her whole body toward Peter. "So we've established that your papa was a rolling stone. I hope you're not going to be a chip off the old block. I've heard about your track record at work."

"I'd like to think I'm nothing like my father," Peter insisted firmly.

"You say that now, but your actions say something different. Rachael told me how you always have a woman at work thirsting after you, and you even broke up an engagement! The only difference I see is that your father marries them first. You just break them up before they become marriages."

The comfort that Peter had felt at this dinner leached away from him the more MiMi spoke. *Is that how people see me?* Peter wondered.

"I-, I don't know what to say," Peter stammered. "I try very hard not to be like my father."

"Mimi," Rachael interjected, voice measured. "I don't think Peter's having fun anymore. He's his own man and can stand on his own merits. To be fair, since we've been working together, Peter has been as good as gold. No workplace extracurricular activities. He's practically been a boy scout."

Peter felt his heart warm at even that slight defense from Rachael.

"Oh, I'm sorry, Peter. I didn't mean to make you uncomfortable. Believe me, I wouldn't have invited you over if I didn't think you were good for my grandbaby. Shoot, I think she'll be good for you too."

"Bess, let the boy eat. Quit matchmaking. He's gonna miss out on this good hot food if you keep putting him on the spot like that," Pops added. "Let me tell you, Peter, you want to enjoy this good food hot! Ain't nothing better."

"He's right. I didn't make this food for you not to enjoy it," MiMi Palmer said.

They tucked into their meal, and the lighthearted mood returned to the evening.

Chapter Eighteen

DISHES AND DANCING

"Thank you so much! Everything was fantastic!" Peter said enthusiastically. "Please, let me help with the cleanup."

"You don't have to do that, Peter," Rachael suggested. "I always take care of cleaning up on family dinner nights."

"Please, let me help you. It's not often I get to feel like I'm a part of a loving family like this. I want to help."

Peter and Rachael washed the dishes in companionable silence, moving in tandem as if they were designed to work together.

"Peter, I," Rachael began

"Rachael-"

Their words overlapped, and both began to chuckle. "Ladies first."

"I'm glad you recognize a lady when you see one." Rachael nudged him with her shoulder and gave him a big grin. "Anyway, I just wanted to say you were a really good sport tonight. I'm sorry if Mimi's questions made you uncomfortable. You rolled with it, though. I respect that."

"Wow. Stop the presses!" Peter put down the platter that he was drying and turned his full gaze on Rachael. "Did *the* Lady Rachael Palmer just say that she respects me? The Asshole from Work? Hang on... I may need to get some eyewitnesses. No one will ever believe this." Peter tried to go out to the living room.

"Slow down there, buddy. Let's not get carried away. I'm just saying I appreciated how you accepted the situation and even tried to answer her questions. I respect the hustle... not the hustler," Rachael teased and blew a puff of suds towards his face.

"Ah, you see... You just wait. I'm winning you over. C'mon. Admit it. You like me a little bit." He took a bit of the suds and booped the tip of her nose.

"You know, last time you did that, I took it as an open invitation to fight," Rachael giggled.

"What if it is just an open invitation, period?" Peter asked. His voice was still tinged with laughter but there was something else rumbling underneath it.

Rachael glanced over at him and arched her eyebrow in response.

"How about you keep drying and tell me what you were going to say earlier."

Peter gave her a knowing grin and resumed his kitchen duties.

"I just wanted to thank you for sticking up for me. You didn't have to do it, and I appreciated you looking out for how I was feeling. People don't usually do that sort of thing for me."

"Can I be honest with you, Peter?" Rachael asked.

"From you? That's all I ever want," Peter confessed.

"You spend too much time leaning on your looks and your sparkling personality. No one ever gets to see the real you. It was easy to speak up for you tonight because you've given me something real to work with. I don't know if that's the only depth that you have but for now, I'll take it. Keep giving the real Peter and people will return it back to you. You don't have to always be the shiniest star in the room. I know there's more to you."

Peter took in her words and worked in silence for a few minutes.

"You know you just described my father." Peter shook his head and gave a wry laugh. "He just keeps showing up tonight, whether he's wanted or not."

"Want to talk about it?"

"I wish I didn't, but... He's this ever-present millstone around my neck. He's just so needy... attention, money, time. He sees me as the solution and cause of all of his problems."

"Really? What do you mean?"

Peter went on to tell her a little bit about Evan's financial woes.

"...So, it has only gotten worse over the years, but I have become his personal ATM."

"You know that's messed up, right? You don't actually have any financial responsibility for his children if he's not even trying for himself. I feel like giving him a piece of my mind!"

This woman, Peter thought, *she is so passionate and fiery. I need this in my life. I need her.* Peter smiled inwardly. Right then and there, he made a decision that Rachael was going to be his woman, not just for teasing and hot elevator kisses. She was going to be his in all ways.

Chapter Nineteen

WEEKEND AT HENNIE'S

From: Kathy Starnes (on behalf of Hendrick Pfeiffer, CEO)
To: WCP Department Lead Distribution List
Subject: Quarterly Leadership Jam (Session Three Update)

Dear Colleagues,

After the tremendous success of our last Leadership Jam, our next session is going to be extra special. Please come prepared with the essentials for a weekend getaway. This weekend will be all about connection, vulnerability, and willingness to expose ourselves on another level.

Please be prompt and ready to leave at 2:00 P.M. this Friday afternoon. Sunscreen and toiletries will be provided.

Sincerely,
Hendrick Pfeiffer, CEO
WCP Industries.

* * *

Insta-chat Kane: Little Bird
Insta-chat Palmer: *eye roll emoji* What's up, Kane?

Insta-chat Kane: Looks like we're going to have a weekend getaway

Insta-chat Palmer: It's still a work event. Don't get any ideas.

Insta-chat Kane: All I have are ideas. You like my ideas.

Insta-chat Palmer: Okay now.

Insta-chat Kane: *innocent emoji*

Insta-chat Palmer: Cute.

Insta-chat Kane: I certainly am.

Inta-chat Palmer: Ugh. I can't with you right now. I actually have work to do. Unlike some executives I know.

Insta-chat Kane: Okay. Will I see you at Pops and Mimi's on Wednesday?

Insta-chat Palmer: Um. They are my grandparents, so I'll be there. I don't know about you.

Insta-chat Kane: I've been at the last four dinners. They love me now.

Insta-chat Palmer: I can't imagine why. Don't forget we have to meet with Señor Cartagena, too.

Insta-chat Kane: *angry emoji*

Insta-chat Palmer: LOL Pedro is the best. Catch you later.

END OF Chat

* * *

Rachael waved to Chaundra and Casey as they took their map and headed off to their lodgings. She took a deep breath and inhaled the fresh Caribbean breeze. She was feeling refreshed and excited about this unexpected tropical getaway. Of course, she quickly remembered that it wouldn't all be fun in the sun. This was a Hendrick Pfeiffer team-building experience with any number of unexpected challenges. As she stood taking in the expanse of the clear blue of the ocean, Rachael felt a comforting presence behind her.

"The view is almost as beautiful as you," Peter whispered in her ear.

"Peter. MiMi isn't here. You don't have to play into her plans when she's not around. We're barely friends, boy. That's plenty good enough."

Rachael looked around self-consciously. This wasn't like the time they spent together outside of regular working hours. There was a real chance that she would get the same reputation as Kerry if she were seen cozying up to him too much. While she could admit to herself that she was attracted to him, he still just had too much baggage with him. He may have spent most of his time around her these days, but it wasn't enough to negate his past. When they were at the office, she still heard the flirtatious tone he took when he wanted something from a female colleague. He still had Kerry fawning after him and giving her dirty glares at every opportunity. No, she wasn't ready to let her guard all the way down.

"Little Bird. You wound me. But I get it. Once an asshole, always an asshole, right?" Peter asked, picking up his carry-on bag. "Let's go get our room assignments."

"People, hurry and get your assignments. I have some special treats for some of you. So don't dilly dally!" Hendrick Pfeiffer's voice boomed over the beach.

"I'll race you," Rachael grinned and took off at a light run to get to Kathy Starnes, leaving Peter behind.

* * *

Rachael settled into her room, which ended up actually being one of two penthouse suites, complete with its own private elevator entrance. She wandered the massive suite, noting the wall-to-ceiling windows that encompassed the living and bedroom space. The view was amazing. She could look out onto a private beach area with cliffs and rocks from every room in the suite. It was furnished in teak and cool linen colors with a beautiful earth and stone kitchenette with modern appliances made over to look rustic. It was gorgeous. The only worrying aspect of the unit was that there really was not a wall separating it from the second penthouse suite. Instead, it was divided by nothing more than a paper shoji screen that stretched the expanse of the apartment. She hoped that she would be alone on the floor for the sake of her privacy. Deep down, she knew that she hoped in vain. After all, Peter had been on the same elevator.

"Rachael! Are you over there?" She heard Peter's voice call out.

"Peter?"

"Yeah, come over and check my place out. Actually..." He paused, and she saw his shadow moving on the other side of the screen. "That's much better!"

He slid the screen to the side, which activated an automatic recess feature. The suite opened up to its full penthouse potential, revealing near panoramic views of the island. It was so beautiful that Rachael didn't spare a moment to take in the implications of their now shared quarters.

"Oh my goodness, Peter! This is stunning." Rachael said in astonishment. "Let's go exploring!"

Rachael squealed delightedly and grabbed Peter's hand to run over to see the panoramic view from his side of the suite. From there, the beach expanded to pure white sand and the bluest cerulean water. Palm trees fringed the inlet, foliage rising upwards towards the building dotted with the brilliant colors of tropical flowers. At this height, you could see the Caribbean outstretched for miles, dotted with patches of green, signifying small islands. Rachael sighed, staring at the breathtaking view, and found herself resting contentedly on solid, warm flesh. That familiar juniper and citrus scent enveloping her first, followed by strong arms. She wanted to protest, but there was no one around, and as much as she wanted to resist her attraction, she couldn't muster the energy. *Just this once,* Rachael thought, *I'll enjoy the moment and get out of my head.*

Peter rested his chin on top of Rachael's head and murmured, "I'm so glad to be here with you. I'm not sure if I've ever felt this comfortable."

They stood like that, melting into each other for quite some time before Peter broke the silence once again.

"We probably should finish checking the rest of the place out." He slid his hands down her arms and took both of her hands in his. "Ready?"

Rachael nodded and stepped to his side, continuing to hold his hand, feeling how solidly built Peter was all over, down to his fingers. Chills slid up and down her spine, thrilling her senses, her body responding even to this slight contact. She shivered slightly and felt, rather than heard, Peter's deep chuckle. *Dammit, he felt that.*

The surprise of the penthouse suites was that there was only a small futon-style bed in Peter's half of the suite. It was narrow, leather, and stylish however, it appeared better suited to an office or perhaps only for interior design aesthetics. It was evident that he was never going to be able to sleep there. Rachael felt cold settle in her stomach, along with an intense case of butterflies, as she recalled the massive bed on her side of the penthouse. She wasn't going to suggest anything right now, but if things were cool between them and he didn't show his ass when they were out with their coworkers, then Rachael could admit to herself that she *might* be willing to share her space with him.

A text alert from Peter's phone informed them that they were expected for the first team event of the weekend shortly and that they were to be back down on the main beach.

"I guess that's our cue. I'll meet you at the elevator," Rachael said and scampered off to get ready.

Chapter Twenty

RETURN FROM THE LAGOON

"Oh man!" Rachael and Peter burst into their shared suite laughing.

"I can't! I can't!!!" Peter laughed as hard as Rachael. She was wheezing with laughter at this point, barely able to support herself. Peter held her close to his side as they found their way to one of the over-stuffed lounges facing the cliff. Thankful for the support, he allowed their bodies to collapse onto the sofa. Rachael landed on top and faced him with a soft thud.

"I'm sorry. I want to stop laughing, but I can't. I thought co-ed Twister was the ultimate Hendrick Pfeiffer team-building experience," Rachael wheezed with laughter.

"Nope! We stand corrected. The ultimate is Limbo!" Peter chortled, body shaking with laughter.

"Never, never ever in life did I expect to see Mr. Pfeiffer's testicle."

"But out it popped in 3D."

"Poor Chaundra! They won the challenge, but I'm not sure if it was worth it. He actually expected her to shake his hand after adjusting his balls!"

"Do you think she's really sick?" Peter asked.

"Maybe, but I'm 99% certain it came on suddenly and mostly from the thought of touching Pfeiffer's scrote hands."

Rachael snorted with laughter and buried her face in the crook of Peter's neck. His continued laughter caused her body to rock against his. The friction of their skin-to-skin contact brought her up short as she realized that they were both wearing the skimpy swimwear that had been supplied to them courtesy of Hendrik Pfeiffer and WCP Industries. She raised her head and locked eyes with Peter. He had been so much fun tonight. For once, he hadn't thrown any digs at Casey, no snarky comments toward anyone. He'd just been his authentic self— fun, supportive, and gorgeous. She licked her lips as she gazed down at him. Her waves fell down over her shoulder and swayed lightly over his chest. She glanced down, noticing that his nipples had hardened into small, tanned peaks. She wondered what would happen if she rubbed her larger, stiff nipples against his. What would he do if she brought her head back down and bit his full lower lip?

She was a take-charge kind of woman. Rachael didn't need him to make the first move. If anything, she knew that it had to come from her. How else would she know if it was really something she wanted or simply Peter doing what he always did? Going for what was closest to him. Whether she was giddy from the heightened insanity of the team building or because the tension had been building up between them since the day they were partnered together, Rachael would never know. All she knew was in that moment, the only thoughts in her head were *Fuck it* and the knowledge that the man she had been reluctantly crushing on in secret was right in front of her and his eyes were locked on to her as if she was the only woman that had ever existed and found her exquisite.

She rubbed her body against Peter seductively and gave him a wicked grin.

"Rachael," Peter gasped out right before she placed her lips against his, licking and nibbling before pulling that plump bottom lip between her teeth and biting, then she sucked it to soothe the sting she knew that he felt from her teeth. His whole body shuddered as he moaned.

Pulling her body tight against his, he kissed Rachael with abandon, hands roaming everywhere all over her body. It felt like he was trying to map out every curve and crease of her existence. Rachael's legs fell to either side of his as he reached down and grabbed a cheek in each hand and squeezed. Sliding his hands back up and over the firm globes of her butt, he slipped them underneath her bikini bottom, feeling the smooth skin. She ground against him, encouraging his touch as they continued to kiss, bodies sliding over each other at the early stages of a rhythm that would become all their own. One hand stayed in her bottoms as the other slid up her back and pulled the string to her top, releasing her breasts and fulfilling her desire to be free of the fabric. His other large hand rubbed her cheeks, his pink straying further south, encountering her most intimate area. He used that digit to glide up and down her folds while his hips began making small thrusts upward. Rachael could feel the heat rising throughout her body. She sat up slightly, leaving the bikini top to lay on his chest. She wanted to watch him as he got his first glimpse of her body. His eyes danced all over her form, and the grin on his face was both devious and sexy. His abs flexed forward, and as he raised up, he let his tongue sweep along the underside of her breast and then circle her areola. He pulled her nipple into his mouth and gave it the same treatment that she had given to his lip- biting and then sucking hard on the tip. Rachael moaned and moved against him some more. Peter's hands gripped her hips, and he rocked her back and forth over his fully engorged erection.

"You feel so good," Rachael moaned.

"I know what would feel better," Peter rasped.

"Yeah? Show me," Rachael urged.

Peter stood, keeping Rachael's legs locked around his waist, and carried her to the massive bed. He walked her to the bedroom, all the while whispering sweet words to her.

"You are the most beautiful woman. You look so pretty like this. I've wanted you for so long."

The bed felt like it was too far away and too close. The space between reaching the goal and anticipation was tantalizingly sweet. Finally, they reached the bed, and Peter placed Rachael down. She sat seated on the edge, watching his lean muscles ripple as he inhaled deeply. She reached a hand and touched his waistband. Taking her cue, he pulled the square-cut briefs off in a single swipe, stepped out of them quickly, and then fell to his knees before her like she was his goddess. He gave a soft kiss between her breasts before working his way down past her belly button, kissing until he reached her bottoms. He looked up at her, eyes pleading.

"Please?" he asked.

That plea for consent turned Rachael on in a way that she never anticipated.

"Do it," she nodded, waiting to see what he was going to do next.

He placed one more kiss just above her waistband and pushed her back slightly so that her hips had a more upward tilt. Then, using his teeth, he pulled her bottoms down, his hands raising her hips and finishing the removal. Finally, they were both completely bare, seeing each other for the first time as they really were. Peter kissed the inside of her thigh, giving full eye contact.

"You," he rasped. "You're amazing." Then he plundered her V with his tongue like it was the most delicious treat, and he was a starving man being fed for the first time.

Rachael cried out in shock and pleasure. Never had anything felt like this before. It wasn't just that he was skilled. No, skill could never accomplish the completeness, the sensation of right that she was feeling. Her hands caressed his hair and gripped and pulled lightly. Peter returned her cry with a moan of his own. With another flick of his tongue, Rachael was careening. She pulled him up with her as she fell completely backward on the bed. He moved up next to her on the bed and caressed and cradled her body against his as her body began to relax from the sensations.

Rachael caught her breath, chest heaving lightly. She smiled in relief at the full body tension that had ebbed from Peter's attentions. Not fully satisfied, she wanted to give back. Her slightly more aggressive nature took hold, and she pushed Peter down onto his back and straddled his waist. She smiled, gave him one of her looks, and tossed her hair to the side.

"Ready for me?"

"For you? Always."

Rachael grinned and ran her nails down his chest, leaving red scratch marks. She pinched his nipples, watching the way his chest puffed up, as if reaching up for her touch, nipples pebbling even harder than they were before. She bent down and bit his chest. His hips jerked in excitement. He reached for her, but she took his hands and shook her head.

"Just feel what I'm doing to you."

"Okay," he faltered, a brief uncertain look flashed, and then he nodded in agreement and let her lead the way.

Rachael kissed and bit his chest and stomach, inflicting little stings and soothing kisses the entire way. Finding the right balance and excitement, she worked his body into a state of extreme arousal. His erection stood high and proud as she moved across his body. Rachael massaged his hips, kissing the crease of his thigh, hovering so close to the main attraction, and then skipping it to kiss the other thigh's crease. She continued down his legs, massaging, kissing, and biting. Peter's body was trembling with excitement as she tantalized his body, kissing him all the way down to his strong, thick thighs. Her hand caressed his hardness as she kissed between his thighs, heading northwards and working him with her hand. She pumped him until his hips worked in tandem. Peter grasped her hand, and together they worked his body until he screamed in pure delight, lust, and passion. Rachael swallowed his moans with her deep kiss. She felt supremely satisfied.

"So good. You are...." Peter breathed deeply. She watched as his whole body continued to twitch from post-orgasmic shudders. "You are everything."

Rachael preened in his praise. They snuggled together under the sheets and fell asleep in a tangle of limbs.

* * *

Rachael's eyes sprang open. First, she caught a juniper citrus fragrance in the air. Next, she felt the satisfied glow of her own body. Then she glanced to the left and saw Peter's beautiful naked form sprawled next to her. His arm was tucked around her body. Second, her mouth formed a silent "oh" as she internally screamed. What had she done? And why did it feel so right?

* * *

Peter lay next to Rachael, his eyes closed, despite being awake and listening to her breathe as she slept. He refused to open his eyes lest the memory of everything that transpired prove to be a dream. Peter had known that he wanted Rachael for such a long time. He knew that she was the endgame for him. Nothing had driven that point home as intensely as the last night's experience. It wasn't as though Rachael had been his first. Hell, they hadn't even had full-on sex. Yet, he felt reborn. His time with Rachael last night felt like he had fully awakened to what sex, intimacy, and connection could be like with someone that he truly cared about and esteemed beyond what he could get in the moment. Rachael was so much more than any woman he had ever been with. He wanted to feel like this forever. It was time to level up his life. Peter was sprung and Rachael was his it for him.

Chapter Twenty-One

MOTHERS KNOW BEST

Peter sat in his office ruminating on the previous weekend's events. Rachael had briefly been distant after that first night together. The last few days had been tense for him. He wanted to spend as much time with her as he could but the demands of the events and her skittishness had made it difficult. She wasn't cold to him exactly. Not at all. She was prickly as ever, even a little flirty. However, every time she caught herself flirting or looking at him he could see that she looked scared, like she wanted to retreat. Two days into the event, she had left and found her way to Casey and Chaundra's cottage. On instinct, he went looking for her. He overheard Rachael say to Chaundra that she liked him. He couldn't dismiss the dismay and trepidation in her voice, but it did give him hope. Despite her worries about his past and who he had been, there was hope. He just had to figure out how to overcome her concerns.

His phone rang, and his mother's smiling face flashed across the screen.

"Hi, Mom!"

"Hey, baby! I haven't heard from you in a while and wanted to hear your voice." Magda's voice came through the phone like an embrace. "How have you been? Everything okay?"

"Yeah. I'm good. I don't know how you do it though," Peter replied.

"How I do what?"

"You always seem to know when to call when I need you. You must have a sixth sense."

"You're always going to be my baby. Nine months of symbiotic connection doesn't just go away. Tell me what's on your mind."

Peter waited for a beat, trying to formulate his thoughts.

"A lot has been happening over the last few months. I've been part-nered with a woman at work for special assignments. I've publicly made an ass of myself. I caused a physical, actual fight at a work event, Mom. I've been jealous of one of my clients. Dad's been calling me for money, surprise surprise." He paused again to catch his breath and to say the words that he dreaded the most. "I've tried really hard, Mom. I don't want to be like him, but I keep getting shown all of the ways that I'm just like him."

"Oh, honey. You're really going through it. Why don't you meet me for lunch today? Or better yet, if you can, take the afternoon and spend it with me?"

"I'd like that. Let me clear my schedule, and I'll meet you at home in about an hour."

* * *

Peter arrived at his mother's colonial-style house and found her waiting at the door for him. She greeted him with open arms and a big kiss on the cheek.

"Come inside. Lunch is ready."

They sat down and started eating. Being in his childhood home was so reassuring, especially now that Magda had kicked Evan out for the final time. The only trace of him lay in the photos hanging on the walls of himself and the twins, Darcy and Dara. Genetics couldn't be escaped, Evan's features were everywhere.

"It's so nice to have you home. You should stop by more often,"

Magda said, then grinning, she raised her eyebrows at her son. "Tell me about your girl!"

Peter couldn't help the bashful grin that crossed his face. He never talked about the women he was with to his mom. What was the point? They were fleeting. He knew it, they knew it and that was how he always liked it. Get in, get out, get what you need for the moment, and move on. Only now, with Rachael, that was good enough for him.

"She's great. Her name is Rachael. We've been working together all year. She is so smart and funny. She's unique with her sense of style and love for her family. You'd love her grandparents. Her MiMi is hysterical and says it like it is. I feel like I've fallen for her family almost as much as I've fallen for her."

"You've already met her family? Yet, this is the first that I've heard about her. How is that possible?"

"Mimi Palmer has skills." Peter laughed and then told her the story of meeting them at the drugstore.

"Anyway, I want to show Rachael that I'm worthy of her. I'm all in on this. I'm afraid I've spent so much time being like Dad..." He trailed off and shook his head.

"Other than being devilishly handsome, and fifty percent of that comes from me, you are *not* like your father. I can see how you think that you are, but fundamentally, you are not the same. He's driven by selfishness with glimpses of a good man. You, my darling, actually are a good man with some misguided selfishness that seeps in once in a while."

Peter arched an eyebrow. "Really, Mom? I'm not getting much of a distinction here."

"Believe me, the distinction is huge. Massive. Look at how you help out with all of your siblings. I know that you think you do that because your father asks you to help out, but that's not why you do it. From the day that you knew each one was coming, I watched the excitement on your face grow until you were able to hold them in your arms and introduce yourself as their big brother. You have always been there for your family, whether it was convenient or not. I never worry that you won't put your family, your stepmothers, or even your Dad first when it is needed.

Your father only turns on the charm until he gets what he wants. We have all fallen for it. In my case, more than once, unfortunately. At the core of it all though, what have we seen with your father? He puts his desires ahead of every one of us, let the pieces fall where they may. Think about it."

"Okay. I can see that about Evan, I mean Dad. If you know this, why did you fall for him? Twice??"

"Your father is extremely charismatic. I swear, if he had any real ambition, he would have made a devastating cult leader. Instead, he just made a busload of beautiful children. For which I am forever grateful because I got you and the twins.

It's easy to get caught up in your father. He makes you feel like the only person in the world, and there is good in him. There really is. It's just that he can't separate his impulses and desires from what's really important. For myself, we had such history together. You know we got together as teens. Our relationship can be so comfortable, like an old quilt. You just slide under it, get cozy, and forget that there can be something better, warmer out there for you."

Peter laughed. "I'd bet he'd love being compared to an old quilt."

"Right? Ha! I don't think his ego could take it."

"You know he always says that I ruined his career by coming along. He makes me feel like I owe him for ruining everything for him."

Magda's face tightened.

"Bullshit! You are the blessing that made us become real people and prompted us to grow up. I took to being an adult more than he did, apparently. Any failings in his acting career were by his own hand. Perhaps if he didn't flirt with every woman behind the scenes, he would have been able to succeed. He had an excellent opportunity when you were little with a small startup production company, Wild Cheetah Productions, it was called. He blew it all by himself. Went for the producer's girlfriend. That's what happened to his career, not you. HP, the production company owner, fired him on the spot when he saw what he was trying to do. That was his choice and his selfishness.

I had no idea he was making you feel like this. My love is not conditioned on what you can give to me, and honestly, neither is his. He's just a rotten manipulator. I know that he loves you regardless of what he says, but it's up to him to prove that to you. I won't defend his words or actions, but hear me right now- You, Peter Kane, the man, the brother, the son, are worthy of love. Full stop."

"Thank you, Mom. I just want to be worthy of Rachael."

"Then make yourself worthy and be the man I already know that you are."

Peter spent the rest of the afternoon at his mom's, waiting for the twins to arrive home from school so he could hear about their day. As he was leaving, Magda pulled him into to tight hug.

"Listen, I think you should touch base with Caroline or Sadie. Talk to your stepmoms. They may have some insight to share, too."

* * *

"Hi, Caroline," Peter said.

"Hi, Peter! Good to hear from you. We haven't seen you around the house lately. Emma's going to be sorry she wasn't here when you called," Caroline replied.

"I'm sorry, too, but hopefully, she won't mind seeing her older brother stop by at her new ballet school sometime."

"I'm sure she won't!" Caroline laughed. "I have to thank you, Peter. You really helped us out with covering the costs. You are the best big brother ever! Your father talks a good game, but I know he got the last $1500 from you to cover the fees."

"1500? I thought the fee was $5000."

"No, it was definitely $1500. I'll send you a copy of the receipt. Did your dad tell you it was $5000?"

"Yeah."

"Sonofabitch. Peter, I don't know what he used the rest of that money for, but it was only $1500. I didn't even want him to ask you for it. I'm so glad you are nothing like your father. I don't know how I ever got charmed by him," Caroline's angry voice cut through the silence.

"I'm beginning to feel the same way. Thanks, Caro. Tell Emma I love her and will see her soon."

Peter hung up the phone. It was time that he and Evan had a friendly chat.

Chapter Twenty-Two

WORKPLACE CONCESSIONS

Peter spent a lot of time thinking about the conversations that he had with his mom and Caroline. One thing was for sure, he never ever wanted to become his father, who was an emotional blackmailer and, at best, a financially abusive father and liar. He wanted to be a person that Rachael could be proud to be seen with around town and at work. The only way he could really achieve that at work was to face his own actions, namely the Casey Travers situation.

The whole thing had been in bad taste from start to finish. He could see that now. Stealing Casey's fiancé was beneath him and since Casey was a junior executive and he was senior in the workplace hierarchy, it was a serious case of punching down. It's a wonder Mr. Pfeiffer hadn't suspended or fired him simply for causing workplace disharmony. Remembering how he taunted him when he, Rachael, Casey, and Chaundra had all been paired together for the problem-solving Twister event made Peter want to sink into the floor. He had felt like an asshole at the time, but now he saw how selfish he had been. He could see that Casey and Chaundra had something going on when he teased that he wanted to hook up with her. Peter had only said that because he wanted

Rachael but wasn't ready to come right out with it. It was messed up, and he knew what needed to be done.

He checked his office scheduler and saw that he had a block of time open that coincided with Casey's schedule. He had his admin, Lena, set up a meeting for them and hoped that Casey would be willing to receive what he had to say.

* * *

Peter sat in the conference room, twirling his pen nervously through his fingers. He felt completely offsides. Usually, he was on the offensive, ready to take and get what he wanted, but this situation was completely different. He wanted to make amends, knowing full well that his words could be rejected and there was nothing that he could do to make Casey receptive.

Casey entered the room with a file folder and laptop in hand, his face an expressionless mask.

"What is this meeting all about?" Casey asked brusquely.

"I felt like we needed to clear the air—" Peter began.

"I have nothing to clear. I have work to do." Casey cut him off and started to stand up to leave.

"Please, it's not you that has to do the clearing. Please stay. Hear me out for a few minutes."

"Fine."

"I owe you an immense amount of apologies. There's no excuse for the ways in which I have wronged you. I won't disrespect you by trying to make any," Peter began. He made sure that he was making eye contact with Casey. He hoped his expression conveyed his sincerity.

"You're right. I don't want your excuses. We have to work in the same environment, and until these team-building events end, we will continue to be thrown together," Casey remarked.

"Exactly. I know it's too much to ask that we be friends," Peter said. Casey glared at him. "Right, that's not what I'm asking at all. I guess I just want you to know that I'm sorry. I'm sorry for what I did to your engagement, for the way I taunted you, and for the disrespectful way I talked about Chaundra. Clearly, you two have something special going on, and it wasn't right of me to dig at you like that. Truth be told, it wasn't even about you or Chaundra. I just, I didn't know how to deal with my feelings."

"Feelings for who?"

Peter had the nerve to blush at that moment. Casey's eyes narrowed, focusing on Peter.

"Come on, man, you had a lot of mouth before, so come on with it now."

"My feelings for Rachael," Peter stated plainly.

Casey chuckled and then started laughing. Hard.

"You're interested in Rachael? That's perfect," Casey laughed some more.

"What?" Peter asked.

"If any girl was going to be able to handle you and have you dead to rights, it's Rachael."

Peter couldn't deny it.

"Listen, all that stuff with my fiancé is in the past. If anything, I should be thanking you for showing me who Kerry really was. Besides, compared to Chaundra..." Casey's eyes took on a dream quality. "Nah, man. You did me a favor. We're cool."

"Seriously?" Peter asked, amazed that it could all be so simple.

"Seriously. But listen, don't treat Rachael badly. If you think my fists did some damage, I assure you, you *do not* want to see what Chaundra will do to you if you hurt her bestie."

Casey stood, chuckling. "Good luck, man."

Peter stood too and put out his hand. Casey shook his hand and grinned.

"So, how quickly do you think this will get around the office?" Casey asked.

"$20 it'll be around the office by the end of the day today," Peter countered.

"Easy. $25 if it makes it's way up to Mr. Pfeiffer."

"It's a bet." The two men exited the conference room laughing and having a better understanding of each other.

ELEVATION

The elevator doors closed, and Rachael looked up from her cell phone to see who had joined her. Her body reacted before her mind could. She let out an unexpected moan of delight.

"I feel the same way, baby," Peter said. He stepped closer into her space and ran his finger along her collarbone. Her neck was completely exposed, wearing her hair in a high ponytail. He grabbed the ponytail and gently pulled it to the side, exposing her neck even more. He leaned in and inhaled her before whispering into her ear, his lips feathering against her skin, causing goosebumps to rise.

"I want you to be mine. Not just for the moment, not just on the island. All mine." He gave her a kiss on the cheek and backed away just in time for the elevator to open and for Rachael to give him a flustered googly-eyed look that was seen by elevator's two new occupants- one who giggled outright, feeling extremely satisfied that his plans were working. The other, a blonde woman who glared daggers at Rachael, feeling like she ought to be the one Peter made to feel that way.

Peter simply leaned against the wall, a wicked smirk dancing across his face.

Chapter Twenty-Three

PANIC! (BUT WE AREN'T AT THE DISCO)

"Chaundra! Chaundra!!!!" Rachael whispered over the cubicle wall.

"I'm right here. What's up?" Chaundra walked into Rachael's cube.

"I really need to talk to you. I'm freaking out."

"Okay. What's going on?"

"Not here. Can we leave for a break today?"

"Let's go."

Rachael and Chaundra ended up at a sushi spot about a block from WCP headquarters. Once the tea and miso soup had been served. Rachael decided to let everything out.

"Okay. Remember when I popped in on you and Casey at the retreat a few weeks ago?"

"Yeah, and *you* said you thought you might like Peter. That was so wild."

"Wild it may be, but there is so much more. I know I like him, okay. Like, I know I like him in all ways."

"All ways? Girl. You gave me a hard time for not telling you about a damn kiss. You over here telling me you like Peter in all ways, like in the 'biblical' way? I know you're lying."

Rachael gave Chaundra a pleading look. "Bestie, come on."

"Oh, we're besties now." Chaundra laughed. "Okay, I give. Tell me everything."

Rachael gave her the details.

"So, we haven't gone full biblical, but I can't even be on an elevator with the man now without melting into a pool of jelly. I'm not even sure if I should be feeling this way."

"He literally said, 'I want you to be mine. All mine?" Chaundra asked.

"He did."

"I think you should go for it," Chaundra offered, much to Rachael's surprise.

"Are you serious? We both know he's been an asshole, and what about Kerry?"

"What about her? Honestly, she's the worst one in the whole situation. She was the one who was supposed to be loyal. Plus, I have it on good authority that Peter is turning over a new leaf."

"Wait, what did you hear?"

"Just that Peter set up a meeting with Casey and thoroughly apologized for everything. Casey said he believed he was sincere, too."

Rachael gawked at Chaundra. Chaundra giggled.

"Stop gawking like that Rachael. You're going to spill your soup. Listen, there's a reason you're attracted to him. You're seeing something that the rest of us aren't meant to see. I think it's kind of awesome. You've tamed the beautiful beast."

"Oh my god. You're such a romantic. You remind me of Mimi. She wants the two of us together, too."

Now it was Chaundra's turn to stare. "Mimi Palmer knows him?"

"Um, yeah. He's kind of been coming to our weekly dinner for almost two months now," Rachael mumbled.

"Okay. Now my feelings are starting to get hurt. You've been living a whole double life, and you didn't think to share it with me. Rachael, that man is practically your family. You better stop playing around and claim your man. Before another Kerry type tries to swoop in and make life difficult for you two."

"It's not like that," Rachael said weakly.

Chaundra quirked her eyebrow at Rachael.

"Fine. I guess it is like that," Rachael sighed noncommittally.

"Yup. Now, let's eat this sushi and get back to the office before someone notices we've been gone longer than usual. It's so good!"

"It is delicious. Who would have thought Mr. Pfeiffer's team building would lead to your relationship and my.... Entanglement, I guess?"

Chapter Twenty-Four

EVAN KNOWS, THAT'S NOT THE WAY IT SHOULD BE

Peter had sat on the information that he received from his stepmom, Caroline, for several days, trying to convince himself that it didn't mean what he knew it meant. He wanted to think better of his father, but it was time to face up to the fact that his father had been abusing him financially for years and, in turn, causing him deep emotional trauma. Peter wanted to come to Rachael as a man, standing in his own grace, fully acknowledging that he had things to work on and had a plan in place. One of those steps was dealing with Evan.

Peter sat placidly as the phone rang, waiting for his father to pick up. It was paramount that he approach the situation with as much calm and ease as possible. The only way he was going to be able to get Evan to speak freely was to play the situation correctly. Make it comfortable for him, lull him into a false sense of security, and get him to feel comfortable opening up, then BAM! Peter was going to let the hammer drop on his dad and let the pieces fall where they may. At this point, Peter really didn't care as long as the abuse stopped.

"How's my best boy!" Evan answered the phone, a smile evident in the tone of his voice.

A twinge of guilt passed through Peter. His dad sounded so happy to hear from him. He wanted to sit in that sensation and live there forever. He shook his head and swirled his tumbler glass of whiskey. He had to hold fast if he wanted the trouble to end. No more was he going to be made to feel worthless by his father's words, and was not going to be held hostage financially.

"I'm good dad. Really good. I met a woman." Peter was proud to tell him about Rachael. He wanted to tell every person he saw about the blue-haired beauty that he was falling deeply for.

"Oh, that's great son. Remember what I've taught you. Don't get caught up the way I have, just have fun with them. You don't need the baggage of children. They're cute to look at but at some point, the fun ends, and they just become nothing but needy weights holding you down."

"Gee, thanks, Dad. Glad to hear how you really feel," Peter tried to keep the frown out of his voice.

"Oh, don't get fussy. You know I don't mean you. I don't mean it like that. But my life did change dramatically. No more acting for me. I had to get steady work." Evan sighed. "I'm just saying you won't get to live the life you planned for yourself if you get too wrapped up in kids and a family."

"Noted," Peter rasped. After that ramble, he was less inclined to give Evan too much detail about Rachael. He didn't need her tainted with his father's negativity. Play the game. "When you're right, you're right, Dad. Speaking of kids bringing you down, I can't believe Emma's classes cost $5000. They just nickel and dime you, don't they?"

"Indeed. Actually, now that you mention it, the school wants another $500."

"Oh really? Maybe we should take her out of that academy. I'm sure we can find another one that isn't always looking for more money. I'll send them an email now to find out what they need more money for and let them know we're going to switch schools."

"Wait, wait. Don't do that," Evan said quickly. "I may have the total wrong. Let me handle everything. After all, she loves this school so much. We don't want to let her down."

"Dad. What's the money really for? I know it's not for the school."

"What are you talking about? Of course, it's for the school."

"I mean that I spoke to Caroline. I have the school receipts. I know that you haven't been using all of the money you keep asking for Emma. Why are you stealing from me?" Peter couldn't hold it together any longer and his anger came roaring out. His hurt was palpable.

"I, I need it. It's for all you kids. I'm not stealing from you. I'm trying to build something."

"What are you trying to build? Why is it so shady that you have to lie to me?"

"Don't call me a liar, boy. I'm not lying. I said the money was for your sister, and it is. It's for all of you kids. I'm going to build my own production company if you must know."

"I must. You've been scamming me for years. Your own son! I would have given you anything, Dad, if you had just been honest with me. Instead, you've chosen to manipulate and lie to me. You made me feel like your life was all my fault. You said I basically had to pay you back for what I took from you for being born!" Peter's voice pitched an octave higher as the pain inched up his throat, threatening to release itself as a sob. "Now, I have the chance at love, and I'm not carrying *your baggage* with me. I refuse to be like you."

"Son, son.... Calm down!" Evan shouted back. "I never did any of those things to you."

"Yes. You did. Hear me now, *Evan Kane.* I will always be your son from this moment forward. I am done. I will not be giving you money. I will not help you to support my siblings, and I abso-fucking-lutely will not let you emotionally blackmail me. You even start to play your games, and you won't hear from me again."

"What, what about your sister's classes?" Evan stammered.

"I will only deal with Mom, Caroline, or Sadie directly. Never through you. Do you understand?"

"Come on, don't be that way."

"Do. You. Understand?"

"I got it—"

"That's all I need from you."

Peter hung up the phone and gulped down his glass of whiskey. It was done.

Chapter Twenty-Five

KERRY'S CHOICE

Rachael hopped off of her scooter and detached her bag from the back of the bike. She strapped the bag to her back and managed to carry her smoothie in one hand and her helmet in the other as she walked towards the front doors of WCP. Today was that she would have to meet with Peter, Mr. Pfeiffer and Señor Cartagena to finalize the results of the side project.

"Yo, Bitch!"

Rachael heard someone calling out and kept walking. "You hear me calling you, Bitch!!"

Rachael glanced around and only saw one other person in the lot and groaned. It was Kerry Dennis. Why couldn't she leave the situation alone? Regardless, Kerry wasn't her problem, and her name wasn't bitch, so Rachael ignored her. She had almost made it to the front sidewalk when she felt someone body-check her, causing her smoothie to slosh out of its cup and ruin her crisp, white shirt.

"I know you did not just touch me," Rachael said, spinning around to face Kerry.

"What are you talking about? I just tapped you to get your attention. I tried to call you, but you're apparently too dumb to listen."

Rachael sat her bag down on the ground along with her smoothie. She faced Kerry full-on, hands on her hips.

"Not too dumb, I'm smart enough to only respond to my name because the only bitch I'm seeing right now is the bleach blonde bitch bimbo in front of me. Now, what do you want?"

Kerry bared her teeth in frustration, making her face into a twisted, animalistic snarl.

"Leave my man alone, you blue-haired whore. I've already told you once. Don't make me tell you again."

Rachael looked her up and down, taking in the whole woman. Her hair was a mess. Her clothes were disheveled and wrinkled. Her once pretty face was dry and dusty looking. She looked her over and laughed.

"Girl, bye. Nobody is even thinking of you right now. Go back to sleep in the car where you came from."

Rachael bent down to pick up her things and leave when Kerry made the choice to choose violence. She pushed Rachael forward, causing her to fall nearly flat on her face. Thankfully, Kerry was unskilled, and this was not Rachael's first time tussling. She picked herself up and came back swinging with her helmet, clipping Kerry in the leg. Kerry fell forward and let out a howl of pain.

"You BITCH!!!!! You stupid cow. I'm going to kill you!" Kerry shouted and started windmilling her arms wildly. Her skinny, yoga-powered limbs held little mass or force behind them but she was swinging quickly, so Rachael had to use her dodging skills to get out of harm's way. "You just think you can take Peter from me? He's mine. He wouldn't want some half-shaved slut like you!"

"I'm the slut? You're the one who had to fuck around and find out, and that's exactly why you don't have a man. You don't have Casey, and you'll never get Peter. You're pathetic, not worth the dust on my shoes," Rachael said and stepped back as Kerry nearly landed one of her wild swings. Kerry's momentum from the missed blow caused her to topple to the ground again. This time, Rachael was able to leave her lying in the street and walk into the building. She went straight to security to report that crazy woman.

"Rachael, baby!" Peter's anxious voice called out to her as she reached security. He was at her side nearly instantly.

"You want to know what happened? That crazy ex of yours attacked me. Right outside of the building. This is the kind of reason I can't be with you. You must not have made it clear to her that you're done with her. I'm not going to be fighting any woman over a man, and certainly not at my place of business. I like you, Peter, but this shit is not for me. I don't play games like that."

Rachael pulled the security door open and left Peter standing in the lobby.

Peter's gut rolled. He was not about to lose Rachael because of Kerry. He turned and walked out of the building and found Kerry standing outside, dusting herself off from her fall.

"Kerry."

"Oh. Hi, Peter, sweetheart! That woman that you've been assigned to attacked me!" Kerry threw herself onto Peter, wrapping her arms around his neck, and tried to kiss him. Peter extricated himself from her, holding her away at arm's length.

"No. She didn't attack you. I know it was you who attacked her. I've already talked to Rachael"

"So you're going to believe that Smurfette bitch over me? After all we've been through. All that we mean to each other?"

"We mean NOTHING to each other. Let me make things as perfectly clear as possible." Peter said, bass increasing in his voice. "I am NOT interested in you. I want nothing to do with you. We were NEVER a couple. It was sex and nothing more. You know it, and I know it. I'm sorry to have ever touched you. It will never happen again. So don't call me, don't speak to me, don't think about me. It's over before it ever started. Get it through your thick skull."

"But Peter, I gave up everything for you!" Kerry whined.

"I never asked you to or wanted you to do that! That was your choice! If I ever hear you've so much as breathed in Rachael's direction, I will call the police and have you locked up so fast your head will spin! I want nothing to do with you. Rachael is everything beautiful and good, something you will never be! I love her! I'll never ever love you. Do you get me? Do YOU understand what I'm saying to you? Leave me and Rachael alone, or face the consequences. The choice is yours!"

Security arrived with Rachael in tow. Security surrounded Kerry and escorted her off the premises.

Peter turned and saw Rachael staring at him.

"You... you love me?"

Chapter Twenty-Six

I SAID, ARE YOU GONNA BE MY GIRL?

The front door to WCP opened, and there stood Mr. Hendrick Pfeiffer, CEO, his assistant Kathy Starnes, and Señor Cartagena.

"What have we here?" Hendrick said, smirking at his employees. "I trust that the trash has been taken out?"

"Raquel, cara mia, are you okay?" Señor Cartagena rushed to her side.

"She's fine," Peter said, stepping in front of Rachael as if to protect her from the overly affectionate businessman.

"Gentleman, Rachael. Let's go up to Mr. Pfeiffer's office and discuss things in a less public place," Kathy's sharp voice cut through.

"Ahem, yes, of course, Kathy is right," Mr. Pfeiffer deferred.

Once in his office, Mr. Pfeiffer sat behind his desk and looked at Rachael and Peter closely. His laser focus was analyzing them.

"I trust that neither of you has allowed that little... foolishness... to distract you from our project?"

"No, sir, I'm all in," Rachael responded.

"Same. I'm focused on the project," Peter added.

"Very good. Well, Pedro, how was your experience with two of my finest?"

"Señor Pfeiffer, Hendrick. They were amazing. Lovely, lovely Raquel. She had become so very special to me. I want to work with her always."

Peter growled. Mr. Pfeiffer giggled.

"And your Peter! He is so passionate. Are you sure you are not Latin? You're very fiery!" Pedro smiled and pulled Rachael in for a side hug.

"So you are satisfied with what you have seen here? Will WCP be able to open up on your Honduras property?"

"Yes, on one condition." Everyone held their breath as they anticipated his requirements. "I need to know- will Peter get the girl?"

Hendrick burst out laughing. Kathy tittered as she transcribed everything that was being said.

"Well?" Hendrick said, looking at Peter and Rachael. "Don't leave us hanging!"

Three pairs of eyes turned and stared at the would-be couple.

"Rachael. I meant those words that you heard me say. I know it might seem like it's too soon, but we've been together, side by side, for months now. First, I just thought you were beautiful and admired you from a distance, going all the way back to the day that you interviewed. If I'm honest, I was a little bit in love with you even back then. Then Mr. Pfeiffer paired us together and I got a chance to really know you. You are so funny and sharp—in intellect and wit. I couldn't help but fall in love with you. Then I got to meet your family and before I knew it, my love grew even stronger. You have a deep love inside of you that you share with your grandparents, and it just makes you even more beautiful. I guess what I'm trying to say is, will you be mine?"

Not a breath was released as everyone turned to Rachael, waiting for her response.

A single tear slid down her cheek, and she quickly wiped it away.

"Peter, I thought you were an asshole!" Rachael laughed. "But you've shown me so much more, so much growth. I can't help it. What can I say? I love you, too."

A whoop of joy and applause filled the room. Before she knew it, Rachael was lifted off the ground and being kissed into oblivion.

Epilogue

ON AN ISLAND IN HONDURAS

Rachael exited the bathroom, the satin robe she wrapped around her slipping off of her shoulder. The fabric was quickly replaced by Peter's mouth.

"Peter! We just got out of the shower!" Rachael laughed.

"Exactly, so we both know we're clean." He reached around and palmed her breast, teasing the nipple by rubbing vigorously in quick little circles.

"Mmm... but we have to meet...." She trailed off as Peter's other hand found her clit and started mimicking the same circles.

"What were you saying?"

"What... mmmm," Peter placed his leg between hers and pushed it to the side, giving him more room to caress her entrance and circle her clitoris. He continued to massage her as she leaned back against him. He sat her down on his lap, allowing her to see the ocean view from where they were seated as he continued to work her body. Just when she could feel her body shifting from arousal to pure enjoyment into orgasmic bliss, he removed his hand, slid himself inside of her, and began pumping his shaft into her. They had come a long way from the team-building experience and were now very, *very* well-versed in what each other's bodies felt like.

"You.." (thrust) "were saying.." (thrust) "that we have to meet... mmph"

"Not yet, not yet... oh, not just yet!!" Rachael screamed and reached for Peter's wavy hair and pulled. The tension of her pull was exquisite and exactly what he needed. Peter began pumping furiously until they were both spent, bodies pulsing against one another.

"Sorry..." Rachael sighed. "I was saying that we will need to meet MiMi and Pops for dinner but I don't think they will mind waiting."

"I don't think they'll mind at all," Peter murmured.

* * *

Mimi and Pops Palmer sat at the table at the resort restaurant, waiting for Peter and Rachael to arrive. Little did the wayward couple know that a surprise in the form of Señor Cartagena awaited them at the dinner table.

"Thank you so much, Señor, for inviting us out here with our grandbaby!" MiMi Palmer said.

"Ah, it is the least I could do for a fellow matchmaker! I desperately wanted to see Rachael and Peter together. I saw right away that they were perfect for one another."

"A man after my own heart!" MiMi laughed.

"Okay, you two, I think Rachael and Peter may have a little something to do with it," Pops chuckled.

"Maybe, but I like to think we made it happen. I don't know why they're running so late," MiMi said.

Both Señor Pedro Cartagena and Pops Palmer looked at each other and burst into laughter.

"Oh, you two!" MiMi exclaimed.

* * *

Rachael and Peter finally managed to make it into their clothes when Rachael noticed an alert on her laptop's screen. She clicked on the email and called Peter over.

"Look at this, honey."

From: Kathy Starnes (on behalf of Hendrick Pfeiffer, CEO)

To: WCP Department Lead Distribution List

Subject: An Invitation

Dear Colleagues,

You are invited to a truly momentous occasion. As a result of our Leadership Jam success, we have a very special occasion to celebrate. Please open the attached invitation and RSVP by the date requested. Your attendance, while not mandatory, is certainly expected.

This is a celebration you will not want to miss. This is your opportunity to see just how successful our team-building enterprise can be.

Be there, or be square.

Black Tie Event, RSVP expected.

Attachment: The Matchmaker's Invitation

Acknowledgments

Thank you to my writing family Octavia Price, Lynette Angelica Sivad, Eliza Lovejay, Leon M.L.H., and The Sunday Romance Writers for believing in me and spending many hours in group writing sessions. Once again thank you to my editor, Tori Moore for encouraging and guiding me along this wild ride of crafting a novel and getting it out to the readers.

Thank you, dear reader, for experiencing another view of the wacky world of WCP Industries. I hope you've had as much fun here as I have. Thank you to T, for being my perennial support system! Sending you all the loveeees!

About the Author

Ruby D. Flowers has been writing and creating movies in her mind since she was a small child entertaining herself while doing chores. She has written several children's plays, performed, directed, acted, sang and even danced (questionably, if not adequately) on stage and film. Her love of comedy, the absurd, and a happy ending has drawn her to romantic comedy. After all, what is living but a series of absurd and unexpected situations that lead us through life and love? We might as well have a laugh at the whole experience.

www.ingramcontent.com/pod-product-compliance
Lightning Source LLC
Chambersburg PA
CBHW052009170626
46808CB00007B/2845